I0817641

SURREAL ICE

SURREAL ICE

Dale Witkowski

Surreal Ice: Book 1 of the Surreal Ice Series

Published by Clovercroft Publishing
ClovercroftPublishing.com

Printed in the United States of America

ISBN: 978-1-956370-85-0 (print)

CONTENTS

Chapter 1

SURREAL ICE

Diffused early morning light broke through the frost-edged window. The frigid air woke Marie before the alarm. *Was I dreaming? Did the pilot light go out in the furnace?* Marie slipped her feet out of the sheets and onto the ice-cold floor. Frost had never formed on the inside of their bedroom window before. Marie's sleep-ladened body crept to the diffused light. The sight that met her eyes as she peered through that window sent shivers down her spine.

Ice covered everything. There was no delineation between the lawn and the road. She had ignored the daily ice for years, but this was too much. Trees and wires were down. One maple tree branch lay on top of the family's Ford Escape SUV.

"Rick, get up," Marie yelled to her husband who lay in bed without moving a muscle. Even his graying dark brown hair looked chiseled by an artist's tool. Jane's handmade quilt was pulled tightly around his muscular back and shoulders.

The shattering of a downstairs window broke the silence. Pounding steps reached Marie's ears as a loud "Mom!" jerked her to attention. Debbie stood at their bedroom door with fear in her deep olive-green eyes. "What's happening?" she cried.

"Rick, get up," Marie yelled again as she embraced Debbie and said, "Let's go check on Bobbie." Debbie was a thinner exact copy of her mom with thick auburn hair that defied styling.

Deb led the way down the stairs to Bobbie's room. Four-year-old Bobbie lay curled up in his blankets hugging his favorite bear, Teddy. His cute flattened nose and small ears were the only signs of Down syndrome while he peacefully slept. Twelve-year-old Debbie sat down next to her brother rubbing his back. "Bobbie, get up. Teddy needs breakfast." His sister was his powerful advocate.

Bobbie's almond blue eyes flicked open. "Too cold to eat," he said.

Marie gently came to the rescue. "Oh Bobbie, a warm breakfast will take away the cold on the inside, but first we need to get warm on the outside. How about two pants, two shirts, and two socks."

Bobbie jumped out of bed in his footed Winnie the Pooh pajamas wanting to change into all his favorite clothes.

Marie emphasized only one pull-up after his trip to the bathroom.

Bobbie began to sing, "One, two; one, two; one, two…"

Joy filled this mom's heart as she watched her precious children. Deb was tall and thin with the Irish coloring of her mom. Bobbie was short with the Latino coloring of his dad. Their love for each other bonded them as brother and sister.

"Debbie, could you help your brother get dressed and then get warm clothes on yourself? I'll be back after waking your dad and cleaning up the broken glass from the entry window." *What caused it to shatter?* Marie swept up the glass and hung an old blanket over the curtain rod before going upstairs.

Rick still lay in the same position. His skin appeared cracked and dry. Marie folded back the quilt and touched his arm. He was almost as cold as the ice edging the window. Her mind and heart raced. *He can't be dead!* A very slow breathing rhythm caused his chest to move. "Rick!" Marie yelled again. There was no attempt at an answer. She shook his shoulder, but he was as limp as a sleeping baby. *I have to get help. The kids can't see him this way.* Marie threw the extra blanket over him and reached for the landline phone. It was dead. Stumbling to her side of the bed, she grabbed the cell phone off the end table. The screen indicated, "no service."

"Mom, Bobbie wants Teddy to be dressed, too. Teddy doesn't have two of everything."

"Just a minute," Marie called back as she quickly pulled on sweats, dried frozen tears, and rushed downstairs. "Deb, I need to go to the Stantons to see if I can use their phone. Ours is dead. Take care of your brother till I get back." *Perhaps the Stantons' phone is live. Perhaps they can help me with Rick.*

"Why doesn't Dad go over so we can get breakfast? Besides, there is a lot of ice outside."

"Just get dressed, Deb, and watch Bobbie. I'll be right back." Marie walked as quickly as possible across the two frozen yards almost reaching the Stantons' door when Deb and Bobbie came out of the house to follow her.

Bobbie was screaming, "Teddy two pants!"

Deb called out, "Mom, I can't handle this, and why isn't Dad helping? I called for him to get up, but he didn't answer."

I've got to get help for Rick, pounded in Marie's heart and mind as she yelled out to her children, "Go back inside, I need to get help from the Stantons."

Bobbie broke loose from his sister's hand. He ran across the ground as if nothing was frozen. "Teddy two pants," demanded Bobbie.

Marie slowed her pace long enough to lift Bobbie up and carry him to Stantons' door. "Bobbie, Teddy doesn't need more pants. He has lots of warm fur. More pants would make him too hot."

Deb managed to drag herself up behind her mom as Marie rang the Stantons' doorbell.

Bobbie must have been mulling over what he had been told. "No two pants for me, too."

Deb's silence and wrinkled brow revealed an unspoken concern that something more than the ice and the cold was wrong. She coached Bobbie out of Marie's arms and told him, "You aren't a bear, Bobbie. Teddy is a bear, and bears like the cold." Bobbie pouted, but at least was silent. The three of them stood waiting for an answer to the doorbell while gusts of frigid air engulfed them.

Ruth answered the door with her dog, Sandy, at her side. Anyone could tell that they belonged together. Both were physically fit with short blonde hair and penetrating brown eyes.

"I pet Sandy? I pet Sandy?" asked Bobbie.

Sandy's tail wagged as Bobbie reached for her nose.

Ruth's husband Howard called from their warm living room, "Tell Marie that we can't watch her kids any more. Her husband hasn't worked for me for a year. She's got to get on with her life and either fix up that house of theirs or move."

Surprise and panic increased Marie's anxiety. *Not worked for a year? How? Why is their home warm? They don't watch my kids much at all. Why is Howard being so mean?* The same disbelief and dread shown in Deb's eyes.

Bobbie piped up with, "I pet Sandy?"

Marie pushed aside trepidation as her crushed heart took in Howard's statements. Rick needed help. She pleaded, "Ruth, I just need to use your phone. Mine is dead. Rick is sick."

Howard yelled again, "Close that door! You're letting in a draft."

Tears rose in Ruth's eyes as she slipped a twenty-dollar bill into Marie's coat pocket. Her tears started to freeze as she closed the ice-covered door.

Marie's empty stomach churned as her temperature rose with angry frustration fueling determination. *Rick is working somewhere even if he didn't tell me about the change. He's unconscious. He's not going to die. He's sick. Howard has to help.*

"Why did Mr. Stanton say that Dad hasn't worked for a year! Why did you say he is sick? He's just home sleeping! Mr. Stanton is crazy. I don't like him." Deb stiffened and clenched her fist that wasn't holding Bobbie.

Deb glanced at their house. Her body slumped as she said, "Mom, look at our house."

It was true that the house needed a paint job. One window was now cracked and broken next to the side entry door. Ice clung to the roof, frosting all the windows and the clapboard siding. In contrast, the Stanton home was newly upgraded with grey-blue vinyl siding and new windows.

Marie knocked on Stantons' door again. Ruth hesitantly opened the door. Howard's voice rose again in the background. "Ruth, I told you to tell Marie that we can't..."

With a steadied boldness, Marie interrupted Howard. "May I please use your phone?"

"What for?"

"To call for help."

"Help with what?"

Marie couldn't explain Rick's condition. "Rick is sick and I need help getting the maple tree branch off my car."

Howard came to the door and stared at Marie's driveway acting like he didn't even see the Ford Escape SUV. He slammed the door shut in their faces.

With resolute boldness, Marie said to her children, "Let's pull that branch off the car ourselves."

"We can't do that, Mom," Deb argued.

"We are going to try." In reality, Marie just wanted to get in that car with her kids and drive to the hospital to get help for Rick. *Perhaps we could also get warm by running the car's heater.*

Bobbie was crying, "Want to pet Sandy... Want to pet Sandy... " Tears chapped his checks, but didn't freeze.

"Stop, Bobbie!" Deb and Marie said at the same time. Tears were in their eyes, too, but they didn't drift down their faces. They froze.

Ice crusted the car. The tree branch stuck to the dented roof. Breaking through that ice was not an option.

Deb choked out a suggestion. "Why don't we try the Meads across the street?"

Bobbie didn't want to move and sat down on the ground. "Teddy cold," he flatly stated.

Marie picked up Bobbie and Teddy. All four crossed the road to knock on the Meads' door. Fifteen-year-old Malory answered, "Hi Deb."

Malory's mom, Cindy, came and stood behind her daughter. "What's the problem, Marie? You know we can't watch Bobbie. When are you going to register your kids for school? You can't keep them home forever. And Malory, close the door. It's letting in a draft."

Quickly, Marie asked, "Please, I just want to borrow your phone. Ours is dead." Malory handed Deb her phone before Cindy could decide whether to help them or not. Deb dialed 911 and handed the phone to her mom. There was no answer, and Malory's phone died in Marie's hand.

Malory screamed at them all. "You ruined my phone!" The door was again shut in their faces.

With no option left, Marie told her children, "Let's go back inside the house." *What will meet our eyes? At least it is warmer than outside.*

Upon entering their home, the phone rang. *How can this be when the lines are down?* Marie's quivering voice answered, "Hello."

Mrs. Winton, are you coming to work today? Any missed days and you will be fired. And you can't bring your children to work with you."

"Um . . .Forgive me, but could you identify yourself?"

"Identify myself! I'm your boss, Mr. Jacobs from Jacobs's Grocery, and if you're not here in an hour, don't bother to come in at all."

I never worked at the grocery store. How could I do a job and take care of Bobbie, too?

Deb and Bobbie were searching for food in the cupboard and refrigerator. The house felt like the inside of a refrigerator. Marie told the kids to eat breakfast in Bobbie's room where it was warmer while she went upstairs to check on Rick.

Rick's body still lay motionless in bed. Nothing had changed since she woke up almost a half-an-hour earlier except for the ice. Marie knelt beside Rick and touched his forehead. His condition hadn't changed. "What is happening to you, Rick? Where have you been working? I don't want to lose you." Marie was too cold to cry. She glanced around the room as if there was an answer somewhere, but that surreal ice had started forming on the inside walls of the bedroom. Things were getting worse.

Their bedroom was the only room on the second floor. It was 16 by 14 square feet with slanted ceilings. The stairs coming up to the room were divided in two along one side of the house to accommodate for the ceiling. They began in the kitchen and ended in a 3 by 5 foot hallway leading to the bedroom door. Rick wanted this room to be a special hideaway just for the two of them. He'd even built two walk-in closets expecting to fill them over their lifetime together. *Would this room become a place for only one of us. NO ... ! Will anyone listen to me? Rick needs help. Rick.* "Please wake up. Please tell me what to do." Marie prayed, "God, tell me what to do." *Will God hear me? I don't really know much about Him.*

A new thought which gave Marie some hope startled her out of her confusion. *Mr. Jacobs called me on my phone. It works.* She picked up the phone and dialed 911. Silence hissed on the line. After minutes of waiting for someone to answer, she called her parents. *Maybe their phone will work. Maybe they can help me figure out what is happening.* Marie dialed 742-9367.

It rang three times and her mom picked up, "Hello?"

"Mom, do you have an ice storm at your house?" *Please don't judge me now, mom.*

"No. You're always taking about ice. It must follow you around. What is it that you need? You know that we love you, but if you were thinking of asking us to watch Bobbie, the answer has to be no. He is too much for us to handle."

"Rick isn't well. He needs help. Could you call 911 and get them to send help? You know the dispatchers."

"Why you married Rick, I'll never know. You should get a job, Marie, and send Deb to school. Take some responsibility and call 911 on your own or take him to the hospital."

Marie controlled her desire to scream at her mom, but she had learned to stuff her emotions inside ever since her marriage to Rick. "My car is frozen, mom, with a tree branch on it. I tried 911, but no one answered." *Why won't mom listen to me? How can she be so judgmental?*

"When are you going to get those kids into school?"

"Could we talk about school later, mom. Rick is sick and needs help and I can't get 911 to work on my phone."

"If 911 works on my phone and you are calling me, then 911 works on yours. Call 911 yourself. You can tell them what's wrong better than I can. I've got to go now. I have a meeting. You can let me know how things work out later."

"Have a good day, Mom," Marie squeaked out between clinched teeth as she hung up.

Deb called from downstairs, "How sick is Dad, Mom? I can help."

Marie knew if Deb saw her dad, she would be an emotional wreck, but she needed to do something to save her husband. Guilt, fear, and hopelessness almost immobilized her.

I refuse to be defeated! If no one was going to help us, then I had to do something myself. Please God, help.

Marie went downstairs, grabbed a thermometer from the medicine cabinet, ran upstairs, and managed to get Rick's temperature. 94.5 degrees. *We have to warm him up without any electricity. Perhaps, just perhaps, there is still some warm water in the hot water tank. Why didn't I think of that before?*

Marie heard Deb starting to climb the stairs. She met Deb at the top of the stairs. "Deb, honey, could you change Bobbie again? I'm going to get warm water from the hot water tank and take it upstairs. The cold is bothering your dad more than us. Right now, I'll need you to watch Bobbie. Get out his special sleeping bag and give him his handheld game." *Thank goodness our hot water tank, bathroom, and laundry room are on the first floor.*

Deb went downstairs, peeled off Bobbie's layers of clothes, and helped him get cleaned up with only a begruntled look in her mom's direction. "I could help with Dad, too, Mom."

"Game, game." Bobbie repeated. He could hear the word *game* if it was spoken anywhere in the house.

Marie spoke to Bobbie as she descended the stairs. "It will be like camping inside, Bobbie. Do what your sister says. Deb, I'll let you know if I need help with your dad." Deb did not appear as excited as Bobbie about games. *At least we had batteries.*

Marie ran the water out of the tank. It was hot. *God if you are real, thank you.* With wash cloths, towel, and water, Marie began the only thing she could think of to help Rick. She placed the pan on the night stand, got under the covers in order to put her body next to Rick, and continuously warmed his forehead, face, and neck with warm cloths. When the water cooled, she carefully got out of bed, went downstairs, and refilled the pan with warm water.

For hours the water in the hot water tank continued to stay hot. Eventually, though, the hot water tank was empty and everyone was exhausted. Rick's temperature was now 95 degrees. He was still breathing. Deb had pulled her blankets off her bed and was now sleeping next to Bobbie on the living room floor. Marie tried 911 over and over again, but only got silence.

Will the ice ever melt? Will we ever be warm again? Will anyone help us? Is Rick going to live? Why does Mr. Jacobs think I work at the grocery store? Marie fell asleep with her body wrapped around Rick to keep him warm.

Chapter 2

NANA JANE

Marie dreamt of days before the ice came. Debbie had always wanted a sibling. Rick and Marie tried for years. Finally, when Debbie was eight, Bobbie was born. They received no congratulations. Instead, they received two sympathy cards. Relatives were silent, except for Rick's mom, Jane, who bought every baby boy outfit she could afford. Jane's thoughtfulness could not wipe away the rejection in Marie's heart. That's when the ice started. At first, there was just a little framing of ice on the rose petals in the yard. Debbie picked the roses and brought them inside. The ice melted and the flowers didn't wilt inside their home. They miraculously thrived.

The Winton home was a warm sanctuary for Marie and the kids. She had been a teacher's aide at Washington Elementary School, but quit to be home with Bobbie. The staff said a few negative things to her face, but mostly their thoughts were revealed in expressions and actions. Ice began to form at the school. It was just a little on the baseboard behind Marie's desk. One aide asked, "Why didn't you have an abortion when you found out that your baby probably had Downs?"

A teacher stated, “You’ll never have an empty nest.”

The young secretary said that she would never have a disabled baby and then remarked, “He’ll be a burden on us all.”

There were of course some who supported Marie. They cooed at Bobbie saying, “Those blue eyes sparkle.” Bobbie loved hugs and cuddling. Yet, the negative statements wore on Marie’s heart more than the positive ones uplifted her. She began to view everyone as negative. Bobbie needed her, so Marie became a stay-at-home mom and secluded herself from social contacts.

It wasn’t that easy for Rick. He got a second job so that Marie could stay home. The long hours caused him to be tired all the time. His happy, easygoing personality suffered. Sometimes, even smiles and hugs from Bobbie didn’t alleviate a growing depression.

The Wintons used to have people over about once a week. Now, very few people visited them, especially as Bobbie turned three and then four. Cousins teased Bobbie for needing pull-ups. Rick’s brother, Kevin, and his wife, Sophia, apologized for their children’s behavior, but started to stay away. Marie didn’t reach out to relatives or friends either.

Some of the people Rick worked with were really outspoken in thoughtless comments.

“An abortion could have prevented all your problems.”

“It isn’t good for your daughter, Debbie.”

Ice began to form like frozen dew on the grass in their yard which never melted. At least they didn’t have to mow, but neither could they enjoy being outside. Rick had spent so much time making a yard of thick grass edged by begonias, alyssum, creeping thyme, roses, and lavender. Weeds intermingled with the flowers now, and everything was covered with icy water droplets. Icicles hung off the roof. There was only one season in their yard: winter. The neighbors around the Wintons experienced four seasons. Marie didn't understand why Spring, Summer, and Fall never came to their property. However, their home was warm and secure inside until today.

Deb had trouble at school, too, especially from neighborhood boys. "Your brother is stupid," was one of their typical teases. Some asked, "Why do you hang out with your family so much?" Ice began to cover Deb's backpack. Deb asked to be homeschooled at the age of 10.

Marie chose to ignore the ice. This was home. They had shelter, food, and each other. Rick, though, couldn't overlook the destruction the ice caused. He frantically chopped at it on the roof only to see it come back. Even his tools began to freeze. The ice built emotional frustration between Marie and Rick. They both refused to seek a solution and stubbornly denied the problem or fought against it.

Bobbie, the one everyone complained about, was the joy of their lives. His smile and laughter warmed hearts even when he demanded his own way.

Marie's dream was suddenly interrupted when the smell of spaghetti sauce wafted upstairs and into her room. Marie jerked up thinking everything had been a dream. "Rick, wake up!" Rick remained cold and unresponsive. Marie covered him with the blankets and went downstairs to investigate.

Before Marie got to the bottom of the open stairway, she saw Debbie and Bobbie sleeping next to each other on the living room floor. Their blankets were covered with ice. Marie raced down the rest of the stairs and over to her precious children. She stooped over them scraping at the ice with her bare hands and yelling.

"Bobbie, Debbie!" They both opened their eyes and crawled out of their comforters as the layer of ice cracked apart. Marie pulled both children into her arms. Bobbie was warm. Deb was cold.

A familiar voice called from the kitchen. "Dinner is served." *Had we slept that long?* Rick's mom stood by the stove with her back facing Marie. Marinara sauce simmered on the stove and spaghetti drained in the sink.

As Rick's mom turned around, she smiled at her family and said, "The food is ready." Bobbie immediately ran to his chair and climbed up onto it.

"Jane, how did you know to come? I didn't call you because of Lee."

"Lee told me to come. It's about the ice, right? The ice has attacked us at various times, too. I'm here to help you and feed you." Marie was still shaking from seeing the ice on her children. *Could Jane help? And how did Jane cook without running water?*

"How did you make the spaghetti, Jane?"

I called Grey's Convenience Store and had them deliver bottled water, spaghetti sauce, and matches."

"I didn't know they deliver."

"They don't. I know the owner and convinced him to make an exception. Now, no more questions."

"Bobbie, stop," Deb shouted. Bobbie had a handful of spaghetti in his hand ready to eat.

Jane came to the rescue. "Bobbie, would you like some sauce with those noodles? Put them on this plate and I'll give you some sauce." Bobbie obeyed. He did love to eat.

Deb, however, stood in the kitchen crying with tears turning to ice. "I can't stand this anymore," she whimpered.

Jane put her arm around Deb's shoulders. "This is hard and you have been a big help to your mom. You are a strong young lady, Deb. We're going to fight this problem together and not let the ice overcome us. Our hearts and tummies sometimes need warming up, too. Have some spaghetti. There were tears in Jane's eyes, but they didn't freeze.

Bobbie's voice brought all of them to the immediate moment. "Nana, want sauce."

Deb broke into laughter. Spaghetti noodles were half on Bobbie's face and half on the plate. Jane added sauce to the noodles on Bobbie's plate while Bobbie pulled noodles off his face and put them into the sauce.

"Jane, how did you know to come just at the right time?" Marie asked.

Jane whispered, "Rick called about 6AM and asked me to come as soon as I could. He felt afraid for you and Deb and Bobbie. Rick and Lee were so close. They let all the negative comments and actions of people build up inside. Their beautiful warm hearts started to freeze. Lee's heart is warming up again, Marie. His eyes sparkle just like they used to. Today, he told me to remember the Light and go to Rick. Tell Rick to remember the Light."

Marie's eyes stung with frozen tears. All the events of the day filled her with sorrow, frustration, and loss. *What secrets is Rick keeping from me? Why did he call his mom, instead of waking me up?* Marie couldn't hold everything inside any longer. "Rick's been cold and motionless since this morning. I'm so afraid, Jane. His body is upstairs in bed. I couldn't get any help."

Deb and Bobbie heard their mom and rushed to the stairs. Jane hobbled behind them as Marie shouted, "Stop!" *Our children shouldn't see their dad like this.*

Bobbie and Jane had to take the stairs more slowly. Deb was in the bedroom screaming, "Daddy, Daddy, Daddy!" Marie couldn't get past Jane and Bobbie.

As soon as Bobbie entered the bedroom, he crawled up onto the bed and laid next to his dad saying, "Daddy cold." Bobbie tried to pull the blankets around his dad more. Jane helped Bobbie. Deb crumbled into a pile on the floor with ice starting to cover her shaking body.

"No," Marie cried as she shook Deb even though her hands burned from the cold. "Remember to fight. Remember the times your dad made you laugh. Have hope!" Slowly the ice melted and just as slowly some warmth returned to Deb's body.

"He's unconscious, Marie," Jane said in a voice choked with emotion. "We should get him to the hospital."

"They won't come and get him. Every time I tried to call 911, the call went dead."

Jane tried to call from her cell phone. She dialed the hospital. "Hello, I need an ambulance to come to 465 Alpine Way, Beckerville. A man needs immediate attention as he is unresponsive."

"What is the man's name?"

"Rick Winton."

"Someone else called about that man. Stop calling for help." The phone went dead.

Jane gently touched her son and said, "Rick, remember the Light. Don't die in the cold darkness."

Marie didn't understand what Jane was talking about, but Rick must have heard her voice as his breathing seemed to deepen.

Bobbie's silence struck Marie as odd. "Are you okay, Bobbie?"

"Light, Light, Light," Bobbie repeated. *Did this little boy know more than the rest of us? He certainly had a great deal of compassion.* Bobbie hugged his daddy, jumped off the bed, and ran and slid down the stairs stumbling a couple of times.

Deb, recovered from the ice episode, ran after him yelling, "Stop!"

Marie followed her children to the top of the stairs to see where they were going. In a few minutes, Deb and Bobbie emerged from Bobbie's room with Teddy. Deb was smiling as she held her brother's hand while climbing the stairs. Bobbie dashed into the bedroom as soon as Deb let go. Marie and her daughter were right behind him. Deb knew Bobbie's plan. Marie continued to wonder. Bobbie headed straight for the bed and his dad with Teddy.

Bobbie pushed Teddy down under Rick's arm and commanded his favorite toy, "Teddy hug daddy."

Tears rolled down Jane's face. Tears froze in Marie's eyes.

"What is the Light, Jane?" Marie asked. If it could save her husband, then she had to know.

Chapter 3

THE LIGHT

Jane shared what she understood. "The Light is all around us, but He doesn't come from the sun or planets or technology. Sometimes, His Light reflects out of people's eyes, but most people don't see His Light or hear the wind that sometimes brings His Light. He is the only thing that will dispel the frozen darkness."

"Where do we find this Light? Is it a person or a thing?"

"He is greater than a person and has authority over everything."

In contrast to Jane's confidence in the Light, her furrowed facial expression and shaking hands which hung at her sides revealed fear.

Ice now covered one whole wall of the bedroom next to the bed. Marie went to the window just as she had done that very morning and looked outside. Something else hit her that she hadn't noticed earlier that day. No one was outside. No plows came through. No electric maintenance vehicles came to fix wires. This surreal world didn't seem to affect other people.

Lights were on in their houses. A few dogs were outside running around in their yards, but all Marie heard was silence. All Marie saw was ice.

Bobbie, tired of being in the bed, said, "Light, Light, Light" again and jumped to the floor. Instead of heading downstairs, he ran to Nana and hugged her swollen purple legs.

"Innocent, unbridled love reflects the Light," Jane said as she patted Bobbie on his back.

"Jane, if Rick called you so early, why did it take so long to get here?"

"Our car is in the shop. I walked."

"Oh, Jane, that is why your legs are so swollen. You live five miles away."

"I am determined to help you. You are my family." Jane noticed the wash cloth and towel hanging over the dishpan. She seemed to be silently lost in thought as if she was praying.

What is prayer anyway? Is God really listening? Is God real? Who or what is this Light? I'm so tired and confused.

"Marie, you have a gas stove and there are more jugs of spring water in the garage from Grey's grocery."

Jane didn't have to say another word. Marie pulled a chair next to the bed and told Jane, "Sit down. I will bring warm water up so you can bathe Rick's head with some warmth. I will also bring up a footstool for your feet."

Bobbie let go of Jane's legs and said, "I wash Daddy, too." Jane sat down by her son while Bobbie again got up on the bed next to his daddy.

Deb felt isolated. She despondently leaned against the frozen wall.

Despite Marie's lack of understanding the situation, she encouraged her daughter. "Deb, we need to help Jane and your dad. We can't give up."

Jane looked at Marie intently, "Tonight we'll work on keeping Rick warm, but, Marie, you and Deb have to go and search for the Light tomorrow morning. Bobbie can stay with me. We'll keep trying to call for help and keep watch on Rick. We'll stay up tonight while you and Deb get some sleep."

"But . . ." came from Marie.

"No buts."

"Where do we start?"

"Start by dreaming tonight and knocking on doors tomorrow. You could also pray."

"How are you going to watch Rick and us tonight so we don't freeze?"

"I have lots of coffee and games for Bobbie and I will pray. Don't worry."

Bobbie heard his name and games. He sat up and said, "I win."

Jane smiled, "We'll see."

Deb inquired, "How are we supposed to figure out what to do tomorrow?"

Jane said, "Here is my phone. I've got plenty of data. Look for any kind of businesses or facilities within walking distance."

"Why can't we go now?"

"They are closed." Jane's response was true. It made things even more hopeless. In between trips heating and exchanging warm water for cool, Deb and Marie sat down at Rick's desk in the bedroom and searched on Jane's phone.

"I'll draw a map, Mom. I love Grandma Jane, but she is sometimes weird."

Neither Marie nor Deb knew much about the businesses within walking distance. After finishing the map, they gave up.

This makes no sense, Marie thought as she tried again to encourage her daughter. "Somehow, we'll get help."

When everyone was so exhausted that they couldn't make any more trips up and down the stairs with water, they decided to get some rest for tomorrow's search. Marie refused to let Jane sit up all night in a chair. She made up the recliner for Jane and Bobbie. Deb pulled out the air mattress and put it next to the couch.

Marie called up to Jane, "We are setting up the living room for the night. I'm going to lay next to Rick to keep him warm for an hour while you get some rest down here."

Jane conceded to Marie's command as she had been nodding off in her fight to stay awake. She came downstairs with Bobbie. "I'll only rest for an hour, Marie, and then I'll check on you and Rick." Jane set her cell phone to ring in an hour. Bobbie pulled out all the games he could carry and settled down in the living room recliner with his Nana. Teddy stayed with Rick. The thermostat didn't move above 52 degrees. Deb had three warm blankets. Another blanket and Bobbie's special sleeping bag covered him and his grandma.

Marie returned to Rick upstairs. Fog shrouded the bedroom. However, no fog rested on Rick's arm that held Teddy. *Was Rick in a coma or unconscious? How long could he go on like this? He is so cold, and yet that shallow breath keeps his chest slightly moving.* Marie crawled into bed next to Rick determined to warm up his body before returning to the living room to check on the others. Sleep took over her body almost immediately.

Marie's mind slipped back in time. She was five again sitting on the edge of the creek in her backyard with her mom.

Excitement coursed through Marie's body as she said, "Look, Mommy! Look Mommy, there are sparkles in the water."

Martha responded to her daughter. "They are crystal diamonds made when the sunlight shines on the water. If you try to catch them, they'll disappear."

Marie sat by the creek for a long time hoping nothing would disturb the diamonds. Would they be there tomorrow? Day after day, Marie ran to the creek to check on those crystal diamonds. When winter came, fresh snow edged the frozen creek.

Martha said, "Let's go and look for diamonds."

Marie protested, "The water is frozen. How will there be any diamonds?"

"Just come with me."

They bundled up. As soon as Marie stepped outside, she saw crystal diamonds everywhere . . . on snow-covered branches, the lawn, and even on the doghouse roof.

"Wow!" Marie exclaimed. She ran to the creek. "Mommy, look. The diamonds are frozen in the creek. Can I catch them now?"

"No. We need to let them shine where they are. If we brought them inside, they would melt."

Marie's mind skipped ahead to the family vacation the next summer. They went to the shore along the Atlantic Ocean in Virginia. To Marie's surprise, there were shiny diamonds in the sand. Where else would there be crystal diamonds? How could anything reflect light without the sun? Jane said that the Light that people needed didn't come from the sun.

"Oh no!" came from downstairs.

Startled by Jane's voice, Marie woke up and was brought back to her frozen bedroom. She threw back her covers and descended the stairs half asleep.

Jane and Bobbie knelt on the floor hovering over Deb.

"What's wrong?" Marie cried while descending the stairs.

Ice covered Deb's face. Jane tried to chip it off yelling, "Debbie, Debie, Debbie!"

"Debbie!" Marie screamed as she rushed to her daughter. *I can't lose you, too! I can't!*

Jane and Marie continued to yell, "Debbie, Debbie, Debbie!"

Bobbie quietly said, "Debbie."

Deb's eyes opened, but were glazed over and unfocused as if she had had a seizure.

Within a minute, Deb's eyes moved toward Bobbie's voice.

He touched her face tenderly. "Debbie, you cold."

"Her blood pressure must have dropped," Jane said. "It can decrease the blood flow to the brain. That was one of Lee's problems. The cold plus emotional stress can cause it."

"Rick," Marie said as she got up to run upstairs. "I had gotten in bed with Rick and then threw the covers off when I heard you scream, Jane."

Marie quickly covered Rick. Could his blood pressure be low? She called to her family downstairs: "Get up, everyone! We are going to exercise and move Daddy's arms and legs."

Marie run downstairs and shook Deb, forcing her to move and climb the stairs. It took them all awhile, but they made it upstairs and Marie led an exercise program for the first time in her life not knowing if exercise would help or hurt or do nothing.

"Jump if you can, one, two, three . . . ten." Bobbie jumped on the bed. Jane raised her arms. Deb did weak jumping jacks. Marie moved Rick's legs back and forth.

"March in place."

Bobbie kept jumping on the bed. Jane slowly moved her legs up and down.

Deb got into it now while Marie continued to move Rick's legs.

"Bend over and touch your toes ten times."

Bobbie kept jumping on the bed. Jane bent over and touched her shins. Deb reached the floor, and Marie moved Rick's arms, careful not to let Teddy fall.

Their hot air didn't change the fog in the room, but it made everyone feel better and Rick was at least a little warmer. Sun rays were beginning to light the sky.

Marie looked out the window half expecting to see crystal diamonds on the ice, but there were none. The surreal ice never sparkled even in sunlight. It was milky and gray.

"Deb, we have to find the Light. Nana is right. The Light that heals is not from the sun."

Chapter 4

BECKER SCHOOL

Jane spoke in a breathless voice after exercising. "Marie, I'm so sorry that I fell asleep last night. I'm sure Bobbie will keep me awake and active today. Where are you going to go to look for the Light?"

Marie glanced at Deb and then responded, "I want to start at the Becker School for special children. Bobbie seems to have some light in him. Perhaps we'll find the Light there."

Jane prepared hot oatmeal and brewed coffee for breakfast while Marie helped Bobbie change and dress. Everyone was glad that the gas stovetop worked. The oven was not reliable. Rick had planned to get it fixed when they had enough money saved.

Deb put on warm clothes and a snowsuit. It was going to be a cold walk of about two miles. Marie pulled on Rick's snow pants along with all her personal winter apparel. Deb and Marie looked like they were dressed for a trip to the North Pole.

There was very little wind and the sun shot rays through scattered fog. The only difficult part of the walk was the slippery ice-covered sidewalk.

"Deb," Marie asked after a period of silence. "Did you dream last night?"

"Yes."

"What did you dream about?"

"All the ice is my fault. Dad is frozen because of me."

"Honey, that isn't true. Why do you think it's your fault?"

"Mom, I loved the ice-edged roses. Sometimes, I wished for more and then the ice covered everything. When kids were mean at school, I wished that their lawns would freeze like ours. I hated them. Now Dad is going to die."

"The ice came no matter what you wished for, Deb. You didn't bring it. We all get mad at people who say mean things."

Deb listened, but still held onto guilt. Actually, the self-damnation was in both of them.

Finally, Deb and Marie reached the Becker School. In the foyer, a sign hung on the sky-blue wall opposite the office. "The Creator Doesn't Make Junk." Below this sign sat a small sage-green sofa with oak end tables and an oak chair on either side. The office wall had a sliding glass door right in the middle of a glassed-in office. Pictures of children covered every possible space around these doors. Perpendicular to the office wall was the double door entrance to the rest of the building. Above these doors hung another sign. The quote made Marie think of Bobbie. "For you created my inmost being; you knit me together in my mother's womb. I praise you because I am fearfully and wonderfully made (Psalm 139:13-14)."

A middle-aged woman with a name tag identifying her as Meagan approached Deb and Marie. Her eyes sparkled like Bobbie's. "Hello, my name is Meagan. May I ask your names?"

"I'm Marie Winton and this is my daughter, Deb."

"Are you here to ask about our programs?"

"No, I have a son with Downs. He is so happy most of the time almost like he has a little light in him. I was wondering if you could explain what that light might be?" Marie felt foolish asking such a question.

Meagan hesitated, and said, "I'd like you to meet Roger. He is an aide here. While you are waiting for him to arrive, here are some leaflets on Down Syndrome, our school programs, and a parent support group—all of which you can peruse. If you have any other questions, please feel free to ring the office bell." Meagan retreated into the office to call for Roger. His name was announced over the intercom. He reported to the office.

Roger and Meagan entered the foyer together. Roger had the slanted eyes, small mouth, and flattened nose indicative of Down Syndrome. Meagan introduced him, "Marie and Deb, this is Roger. Roger, this is Marie and Deb. They want to know what makes Marie's son with Down Syndrome so happy most of the time."

Roger's smile made both Deb and Marie smile back at him. He reached out his left hand to Marie and his right to Deb to greet them. "Hello. I'm glad to meet you. Your hands are cold. You have the ice."

"What?" Marie exclaimed.

Deb dropped his hand and blurted out, "How do you know?"

"The ice is in people who don't have the Light," Roger simply stated.

Marie's frustration exploded before this gentle young man. "The Light, the Light … What is it? Who is it? How do we find it? My whole world is falling apart. Nothing makes sense!"

Roger held Marie's hand in both of his bringing warmth to it. He said, "You are special and you are loved." Then he turned to Deb with those sincere sparkling eyes and said, "You are special and you are loved."

Meagan spoke to Marie's question, "The One called Light comes from our Creator. He is the Creator's Son. He came into the world to save people from the consequences of wrong actions and thoughts which brings on the ice. He is near to everyone. Roger almost died from the ice before he found the Light."

Marie's attention turned back to Roger. "So, where do I go to meet this Light?"

"He is everywhere. Just talk to Him."

A child was being escorted into the glassed-in office by another aide. She had cold metal braces on her legs which to Marie looked frozen.

Roger shook hands again and reentered the office. He knelt and hugged the little girl. Meagan asked Marie, "What do you see?"

"What do you mean?"

"When you look at the child, what do you see?"

"Cold, icy braces."

"Marie, that's part of the problem."

Deb sprang to her mother's defense. "What is she supposed to see?"

Meagan explained calmly and with genuine respect for Deb, "I see a little girl our Creator made who is special and loved like all people everywhere."

Meagan turned her attention to Marie. "Marie, try talking to the Light and ask Him to help you know Him and see people as He sees people."

It was time to go and search for a person called Light, whatever that meant. It was getting hot sitting in the foyer. Meagan invited them back anytime.

"Thank you for speaking with us," Marie said as she and her daughter rose to leave. Out of the corner of her eye, Marie saw Roger now holding the little girl's hand. They were both smiling.

"Mom, where should we go next?" asked Deb."

Marie's mind swirled with no direction at all. So, she tried talking to this Light. "Light, I don't know You right now, but I need You in my life. Please help me. Show me where to go and what to do."

Deb looked at her mom. "Okay, Mom, that was weird."

"Don't you think all this ice is weird, too?"

Chapter 5

THE P&R COFFEE SHOP

About five blocks away from the Becker School, Marie and Deb came to a coffee shop. Something prompted Marie to go in. Gray ice clung to the façade. "Deb, let's go in to this coffee shop. I have that twenty-dollar bill from Ruth in my pocket. We could get coffee and a hot chocolate."

"Are you crazy, Mom? Don't you see the ice?"

"I feel we should go in. Let's try. If we don't like it, we can leave."

The coffee shop was quaint with artificial flower arrangements on each table and booth. Art by local artists hung on the knotty-pine paneled walls. There was no ice on the inside walls or tables. An ordering counter opposite the entry with glass shelves revealed baked goods. One customer sat at a table in the corner near the door. Cracked ice nearly covered him from head to foot. He scowled, but despite his frozen state, held a cup of coffee in his hand. Deb wanted to leave immediately. Marie convinced her to sit at a booth.

A waitress of about Marie's age approached the booth. "What can I get for you?" she asked.

"One black coffee and a hot chocolate."

This waitress sighed as she said under her breath, "Another cheap customer." *Deb was right. This was a mistake. I don't deserve to be called cheap. What is this waitress's problem? Maybe we should leave.*

The frozen man at the corner table yelled, "This is the worse coffee I've ever tasted. I'm not paying for this!"

The waitress opened her mouth to address this complaint just as the door to the shop opened.

A girl about Deb's age walked up to the waitress and hugged her. "Mom, don't worry about money. Mr. Townsend is giving us more time to pay the rent. He likes us living here and he doesn't want us to be homeless."

Marie's heart thumped with compassion and changed her mind. *This poor waitress was under financial pressure and couldn't make much at this job. Her "cheap" comment wasn't directed at me. It was directed at her situation.* Marie read the waitress's name tag. She spoke to her as she pulled the twenty-dollar bill from her pocket and held it out to the waitress. "This isn't much, but it is a gift. Can I charge the coffee and cocoa?"

Seeming surprised, Sally said, "I'm okay, ma'am. Thank you, but you don't have to take pity on me. I'm sorry for my comment."

"It's not pity. This was a gift to me that I'm passing on to you. And if this shop accepts credit cards, I'd like to pay for that man's coffee as well as my order." Marie discreetly pointed to the frozen man at the corner table.

The waitress said, "Um. . . Thank you, but…"

Her response was interrupted by her daughter who looked at Deb and exclaimed, "Debbie!"

Deb looked up quizzically.

"Debbie, we were in the same class in fifth grade. It was Mrs. Kegan's class."

Deb just sat at the booth and stared at this girl.

"I'm so sorry about the teasing that was directed at you in school. I joined in, but always felt guilty. Mrs. Kegan called the principal, but we still laughed after school. Mrs. Kegan really got mad at us when you left."

The muscles on Deb's face constricted into an angry glare. "Sarah, I hate you. You used to be my friend. You were mean to me and my brother. I am determined never to forgive you."

Anger hung in the air for a moment.

The waitress broke the silence. "Are you the Wintons?"

"Yes," Marie replied.

"I'm Sally McCain. I am so sorry for Sarah's teasing. Sarah felt awful about the way she treated Debbie. Sarah has grown up a lot since fifth grade, especially after her father died. She started talking to the Father of the Light, and she meets with some other people who study the Light's Word to learn more about Him."

Deb's judgment of Sarah softened a bit. "When did your father die?"

"A year ago."

"My dad is dying unless we can find the Light to save Him."

"Rick is dying!" Sally sounded in shock.

Judgment and curiosity rose in Marie before she had any information. "How do you know my husband?"

"For the last year, Rick came in almost every day between jobs. He and Carl, that man at the table, got to be friends. At first, they talked about what jobs they had. After a while, all they did was complain about everything. Rick frequently apologized for the complaining. He told me that he was sorry about my husband's death. Simply showing me compassion helped me continue to heal from grief."

How did Rick have time to come here and not come home? What jobs did he have? What did Sally and this unkempt man mean to him? "My husband is compassionate to others, but has little time at home. Now he is almost totally frozen. We are on a search for this Light person in hopes that He can help."

Sally took Marie's hand. "The Light will help you. He is the Son of God. He is the one Who makes it possible to talk to God."

Marie faced Sally. "I do feel a little jealous when you said Rick came here so much. Did you ever hear what jobs he was complaining about? I'm sorry. I love him so much and I don't know what to do." Frozen tears again filled Marie's eyes.

Sally gave Marie a hug.

"Marie, Rick always referred to you as a good wife and mother. He seemed to be down on himself for not making enough money. Rick talked about work he did at Jacobs's Grocery and a lot of miscellaneous jobs he picked up for people."

Deb got up and said to Sarah, "I'll only forgive you if your special Light saves my dad." *Could my daughter's heart be so hard?* Marie asked herself.

Sarah touched Deb's shoulder. "I can only ask the Light. It is up to Him how He heals people. You are special to me, Deb."

Carl interrupted them. "So, you're Rick's wife."

"Yes."

"Where is he? We always talked about our lousy jobs. He would say how he had to work two jobs to pay the bills and then go home to ice. He said that this was the only place he could sit down without responsibility gnawing at him. You ought to be grateful he came home at all. Sally, I'm not paying for this rotten coffee, and I'll be back tomorrow. Hopefully there will be no drama then." Carl got up and walked out of the shop.

Sally told Marie, "Don't let Carl bother you. He is all alone and mad at the world. Rick got caught up in the complaining. I could tell he loved his family."

"Thank you, Sally. I should leave."

"What about Rick?"

"Can you help him?"

"Sit down. I'll make your coffee and hot chocolate and make a call."

"All right."

Sarah spoke to both Deb and Marie, "You can't go home depressed like this without some hope. Mom knows some people who might be able to help, and I'll keep asking the Light to heal your dad, Deb."

Deb looked skeptical.

Marie was overwhelmed and ashamed that Rick had to find a place away from home to share all his frustrations. She thought about their daily lives. *I unloaded on Rick all the trials of my day when he came home. He used to comfort me. Then he began to ignore me. His time with Deb and Bobbie grew shorter except to criticize them for whatever I might have complained about. How could I judge Carl and Rick when I sought peace in complaining, too?*

Sally brought the drinks plus a hot chocolate for Sarah. A customer came in and Sarah jumped up to help her mom. Sarah took the couple's order while Sally made a quick phone call. After the couple was served, Sarah and Sally returned to the booth Deb and Marie shared.

"Marie, I called the doctor who took care of my husband. He said that he is willing to come to your home after 5:00 this evening. Here is his number. You can give him your address when you call."

"I don't have my phone."

"Here, use mine."

Marie dialed the number. A woman's voice answered, "This is Dr. Willard's office. Can I help you?"

"Sally McCain gave me this number and said that the doctor could visit my home this evening after 5 PM to help my husband."

"Dr. Willard is always doing things for Sally. What is your husband's condition?"

Marie wept as she explained. "He is … unconscious and I can't … get anyone to help. 911 never answers and the hospital won't send an ambulance. He is so cold and still."

"I'm sure Dr. Willard will come. He has helped other people with conditions like this. Give me your address, and I will give it to him."

"467 Alpine Way, Beckerville 55089."

"Thank you. I'll see that the doctor gets it."

"Thank you," Marie said before hanging up and handing the phone to Sarah who slipped it into her mom's pocket. Sally had another customer to wait on.

Deb put her arm around Marie.

Sarah came back to the booth and touched Deb on the shoulder again. "Deb, I'm going to get my friends who trust in the Light to ask Him to heal your dad and to give you and your mom hope. Would you like any of us to come to your house and talk to the Light with you?"

"I'm not ready to believe that stuff," replied Deb.

Marie looked at Sarah and said, "I tried to talk to that Light person and I think He might have led us here. It's weird to think about, but if it is okay with your mom, you are welcome in our home."

"If it's all right with Deb, I'd love to go to your home."

Deb's face contorted into a scowl, but she said nothing.

Marie looked at her daughter. "Deb, let's go. It will take a while to walk home and I want to get ready for the doctor."

"You're walking?" Sarah asked.

Deb found her voice. "That dumb ice made a tree branch fall on our stupid car. I wouldn't walk around dressed like an Eskimo except for my mom's insistence and this ugly murky ice. You can come to our house, Sarah, but don't expect me to be happy about it. And don't talk so much about this Light person. It's creepy."

Deb's remarks didn't seem to hurt Sarah. Instead, Sarah got excited about an idea that popped into her head. "Deb, I can run and get into my snowsuit and walk with you and your mom if that's okay."

Deb's arms were folded, but Marie felt the need for Sarah's company, so she responded to her suggestion. "That would be very nice of you to walk with us if it is okay with your mom."

Sarah wrote the request on a napkin. "Mom, can I go to the Winton's home with Mrs. Winton and Deb? Dr. Willard could bring me home after his visit." Sarah slipped the note next to her mom who was getting an order ready.

Sally gave her the okay with a nod and smiled. Sarah rushed home and was back in less than five minutes which was enough time for Marie and Deb to finish their hot beverages. Silence settled over both of them. Marie was in prayer in her mind. *Please Light keep Rick alive. Please heal him and help me with Debbie.* Deb's stern expression seemed to show her determination to hold onto bitterness toward Sarah and disappointment in her mom.

Marie began walking with the two preteens toward the Winton home.

Chapter 6

SARAH AND DEB

The wind had picked up and heavy snow began to rain down. For Deb and Marie, the walk was slippery and slow. Sarah seemed to have no problem.

Finally, Marie asked, "How come you walk as if there is no ice?"

"There isn't any ice in my path," replied Sarah.

"Can't you see it? "Marie questioned.

"The ice reminds those who see it about all the bitterness and anger in their hearts and minds. Actually, our Creator is showing you the ice, so you can seek to get rid of it. Most people don't see the ice because they don't want to accept their hatred or they want to live their lives their own way without any Light and without the Creator's love and teachings."

"I'm tired of fighting this surreal frozen stuff," Deb complained.

"Once you meet the Light, He will get rid of it. The evil behind the ice can't win."

They walked in silence for most of the way home. Even Sarah felt the chill in the air as they approached Alpine Way. "We'll need lots of people talking to the Creator," she stated quietly.

Bobbie nearly burst out the door when he saw Marie, Deb, and Sarah coming. "Mommy, Debbie, where you go?"

Deb ran to Bobbie scooping him up in her arms and tickling him. Bobbie laughed, giving Deb a bit of the happiness she probably longed for.

Marie was next. "Bobbie, you've gotten bigger in just one morning."

"I big, Mommy."

"Yes, you are."

Jane spoke as the three of them got out of their wet snowsuits, hats, and gloves. "So, tell me, Marie, did you find out anything? And who is this lovely young lady?"

"This is Sarah, a schoolmate of Deb's. How is Rick?" Marie was already heading to the stairs as she spoke.

"We exercised four times during the time you were gone. Bobbie got a lot of bed jumping in. I just moved Rick's legs and arms as much as I could. He still has Teddy under his arm."

Bobbie squealed, "I jump? I jump?"

"Okay, Bobbie, but I want to hear Daddy breathe. Jane, a Dr. Willard is coming after 5 P.M. tonight. Maybe there is hope."

Sarah added, "There is hope. Can I call a few friends?"

"Sure. Jane, please give Sarah the phone."

Before going upstairs, Marie watched Deb drop silently onto the gray-blue recliner in the small living room as if she were all alone in the world. While Marie hesitated between checking on Rick and comforting her daughter, Jane entered the living room and sat on the couch next to Deb.

Marie whispered, "Thank You, God, for Jane," as she ascended the stairs to her bedroom and Rick.

Jane touched Deb's arm, "Deb, what's the matter?"

"You're the only one who is really interested in my feelings, Nana."

"Why do you say that?"

"Sarah is one of the girls who said mean things about Bobbie when we were in fifth grade together. She believes in this Light person who comes from this Creator person and now Mom is starting to talk to Him. Then Mom invites Sarah to come to my house and talk to this Light. What about me? Do I count? Haven't I helped with Bobbie? I know that the ice is my fault, but why can't I fix it? Why is everyone taking over?" Deb fought back frozen tears. Ice began forming on Deb's legs.

"You scared me this morning, Deb. We shook you and called your name and broke the ice off of you. You are important. You are special and you are loved by all of us."

"That's what Roger said."

"Who is Roger?"

"A young man with Down Syndrome at the Becker School."

"Well, he is right. Your mom has depended on you because you are so good with Bobbie. It thrills her heart to see the two of you together. And what is this about the ice being your fault?"

"I just don't want to give up my hate toward people who are mean. I want them to have ice, too."

"We all are mean sometimes. We need to forgive ourselves and other people."

"Not Sarah."

Sarah was in the kitchen with Bobbie making a few phone calls to friends. She hadn't heard the conversation between Jane and Deb but did hear her name. Sarah joined Deb and Jane in the living room while Bobbie was kept busy with a cookie at the kitchen table. She shared the results of her phone calls along with a request. "Several people are going to talk to the Light for your family. Can I do that for you?"

"Do what you want," replied Deb.

Sarah bowed her head and began. "Hello, my Creator. Thank you so much for the wonderful things you have created. Thank you for listening to me and helping my mom. Thank you that Mr. Townsend is giving us more time to pay the rent and for the kindness of Mrs. Winton in letting me come to her home. Thank you for forgiving me of all the mean things I've thought, said, and done. Right now, I'm asking you to send Your Spirit into this house so everyone can know You are here. Please shine the Light here and help Deb not be so sad. Please heal her dad. Thank you for my dad. Thank you for Deb's grandma, too. I love you. In the Light's Name, Amen." Sarah slowly raised her head as she looked at Deb.

Deb remained silent.

Jane guessed that Sarah was hoping for a positive reaction. She broke the hushed moment. "Thank you, Sarah."

Deb planted her feet firmly on the floor and let out a loud groan as she rose from the couch, went into her bedroom, and slammed the door.

Jane spoke to Sarah, "Tell me what happened between you and Debbie."

"We used to be friends up until fifth grade. Then I met some other kids who had time to play after school. Mom was working because my dad was often sick and had a hard time keeping a job. The kids started making fun of people who were different than us. We told jokes and laughed. One day, Deb's mom came to school with Bobbie in order to talk with Mrs. Kegan. The kids saw that Bobbie had Downs. When Mrs. Winton and Bobbie left, they all started behaving like Bobbie; talking in short phrases and repeating them, running toward something that was interesting, and jumping up and down. I joined in because it was fun at first. Mrs. Kegan yelled at us and told us to sit down. She even called the principal. Deb was devastated. She only stared at me. She didn't come to school again after that day."

"Debbie loves her brother very much. That must have deeply hurt her." Jane's normal smile melted into furrowed lines.

"I wanted to say I was sorry, but Debbie wasn't in school anymore and then my dad passed away and I got caught up in feeling sorry for myself. It was just today that I told Deb that I was sorry."

"Are you truly sorry?"

"Yes. I started reading a book about the Light. I learned about forgiveness and that our Creator wants us to talk to Him and trust in the Light. It is all real. I feel love for people now and don't make fun of anyone anymore. I am okay living without my dad even though I miss him."

A spirit of tenderness united Sarah and Jane though they had just met. Jane encouraged Sarah not to give up on Deb.

"Go knock on Deb's door and tell her what you told me. Do you have one of those books?"

"Yes, I have a small one in the backpack I brought with me. Would you like to read it?"

"If I have time, yes, I would. Thank you, Sarah." Jane left the living room and went into the kitchen to start supper.

Knock, knock, knock. Deb's voice came from behind the door. "What do you want?"

"It's Sarah. This is a matter of life and death."

Deb opened her door. "What do you mean? Is someone hurt? Is the ice stopping dad from breathing? What is it!"

"It's you." Sarah put her hand on the door to hold it open. "Why are you letting me control how you feel?"

"You don't control me!"

"Then why do you get mad when I talk or am around you?"

"Because you are mean and I'll never forgive you!"

"I was mean and I am sorry. I'm not like that anymore and I really want to be friends again. I've missed you. I hung out with some mean kids when my dad was sick because I didn't want to go home until Mom finished work. I went along with what they did to belong, but I don't do that anymore. I like you. You were always kind. I don't want you to be like I was, mean and lonely."

Deb thought for a moment. "I'm sorry about your dad. What did you mean by life and death?"

"Hate can make us sad and angry. Happiness is killed."

Deb stood in silent thought.

Sarah asked, "Deb, can I give you a hug?"

"Why would I want a hug from you? I'm fine without your friendship." Deb then shut the door.

The ice that had hidden a view of anything outside Deb's bedroom window melted enough to get a glimpse of blue light almost penetrating through a small circle on the glass. The Light noticed a softening in Deb's heart even though Deb didn't want to let the wall around her heart break apart.

Jane called from the kitchen. "I could really use some help from a couple of girls. Getting supper shouldn't be one old lady's job."

Both girls went into the kitchen. One was holding tightly to bitterness. The other saddened by a former friend who would not forgive her.

Chapter 7

RICK

As soon as Marie entered her bedroom, Bobbie ran to the bed and began to jump.

Marie walked slowly up to Rick's side of the bed and folded her hands around his. "Rick, I depended on you too much. I gave you all my burdens every day and never listened to yours. I love you so much."

Bobbie stopped jumping and sat by his dad. He reached out and put his little hand on top of his mom's and didn't say anything.

They sat like that for a few moments, and then Marie said to Bobbie, "I love you, Bobbie. Your daddy loves you, too. Could you go down and help Nana with supper while I talk to daddy some more?"

"Want Daddy's hand, too."

"You can hold Daddy's hand after supper. Nana really needs your help. She may even give you a cookie."

Those chocolate chip cookies Nana brought with her always helped with Bobbie without exception. It was the first word he learned in sign language.

Bobbie relented and walked to the door. He yelled, "Nana, want cookie."

Jane called back, "Bobbie, I need you to try out these cookies before supper to see if they are good."

Bobbie then made his way downstairs. Deb would be at the bottom of the stairs waiting for him.

Marie decided to try to talk to the Light again. *Maybe something will happen.*

"Light, I don't understand. We see ice everywhere for some reason. Sarah said that you are showing us the ice. I don't like it. It's taking my husband's life and Deb is so sad. I'm afraid it will take hers, too. I can't get better on my own. I can't fix this on my own. I'm sorry for my complaining and for being mad at people. I'm sorry for ignoring Rick's depression. I'm sorry for shutting myself off from others and judging them. Forgive me for being mad about Bobbie sometimes. Please, help me if you can."

Suddenly, a blue light shone in the corner of the room by the window next to Marie's dresser. She starred at this phenomenon. *Should I believe my eyes or not?*

Marie saw a hand reaching out to her from the light. She didn't even ask the question that stuck in her mind. *Is this the Light?* Tentatively, Marrie reached toward the hand with her left hand. She received a sensation of peace and acceptance. Marie felt like this outreached hand belonged to someone who would be with her no matter what happened. The blue light lasted about a minute, but it seemed like a much longer moment in time.

Marie's eyes adjusted to the room. The fog was gone. There was less ice on the walls and windows. Rick's breaths were also deeper. She rubbed Rick's arms, adjusted Bobbie's Teddy, so it didn't fall, and felt Rick's forehead. Though it remained cold, it did feel warmer than it did in the morning. Marie began to move Rick's legs in order to warm them up. Then, she got in bed with him and held him in her arms. Marie didn't have time to dream. She had to help Jane, take care of Rick, and check on Deb and Bobbie before the doctor would be here.

Marie hummed one of their favorite songs, "Heaven" by Bryan Adams. Rick and Marie thought that their love for each other was enough to carry them through their entire lives.

Marie touched Rick's cheek and softly spoke. "Rick, we both need this special love that is the Light, so that we can love each other better. A blue light appeared in our room. It isn't scary like the ice. I think it came with someone called the Light. He came to help us. Rick, I reached out to His hand and felt peace. I haven't had peace in so long. I hope you can reach out to his hand, too."

The bed felt warmer. Marie fell asleep again. This time she dreamt of Rick.

Rick was on the football team at the Beckerville Community College when Marie met him. He loved sports, fun, and fixing things. He was always working on a buddy's car or creating something out of any wood he could find. His dad had a shop in their garage with tools Rick could use. Marie's friends encouraged her to ask Rick for help fixing the old Jeep jalopy which she needed for school. Rick and Marie had a math class together, so, after class she approached him.

"Rick, my name is Marie. Could I ask you something?"

"Sure. Walk with me to the school cafeteria. I need to grab something to eat before my next class. What is it that you want, Marie?"

"I've heard you're good with cars. I have an old Jeep that keeps conking out. It's not reliable for driving to school. Could you look at it if you have time?" Sweat moistened Marie's hands and she hoped her red face didn't show.

"My dad's house is on Ridge Road—67 Ridge Road in town. I'll be home about 6:00. There isn't practice today. Bring it over then."

Marie said, "Thank you," as Rick parted to get in line at the cafeteria. She only found out later that he was interested in meeting her, but doubted that that was true.

Rick's dad met Marie first when she arrived at the garage that evening. "That car, young lady, shouldn't be on the road." Rick and his dad examined the Jeep and told Marie to junk it.

Rick asked, "Where do you live, Marie?"

"Over on Meadow Drive. It's the blue house on the corner of Meadow and Sandy Creek."

"I know where that is. What is your schedule like?" Marie shared her schedule with Rick. "I'll pick you up in the morning, and if you wait for an hour or two after your classes, I can manage to drive you home, too." Rick's dad looked askance at Rick knowing his son was piling more responsibility on himself for a girl he had just met.

Those rides were the beginning of their romance. They were married right after graduation. Rick's uncle's pastor agreed to conduct the ceremony in his church. It was a little building with a bell tower something like church images on Christmas cards. About fifty people were there including family and friends. Marie thought Rick was as nervous and as excited as she was.

Marie's mind shifted to the pastor. His name was Pastor Dan. There was a sparkle in his eyes and something else. Blue Light seemed to reflect from him. Blue Light! Did this blue light have something to do with this person called Light?

Rick actually moved.

Marie reacted: "Rick?" Her mind continued to dream though she was only half asleep.

Rick and Marie started life together in a tiny two-room apartment. They loved it. Marie got to decorate and Rick made shelves, a coffee table, and wooden plaques to hang on the wall. One had a laminated ultrasound image of their first baby, Debbie. They put money down on a fixer-upper when Marie was five months along.

"Rick, how will I be able to help with the house? I can hardly move around our apartment?"

"I've got it covered," he said. Friends Rick had made in high school and college joined him in scraping, painting, and fixing walls and floors. Secondhand oak cupboards were put up in the country kitchen. Rick refinished an oak table and six chairs which sat in the middle of the room, and above the kitchen sink was a large picture window that overlooked the backyard. Marie's dad gave them a refurbished stove and refrigerator. Marie could only watch as her kitchen seemed to magically come together.

Debbie was born when about half of the work was done. Marie called from their apartment. "Rick, I think it's time to go to the hospital."

Rick's best friend, Dave, drove Rick to the apartment and to the hospital as he didn't trust Rick to follow any road signs. Dave waited with Rick for the news.

"Mr. Winton, you have a healthy baby girl. You can see your wife and child for a few moments now," reported the nurse.

Marie could never forget Rick's words when he came into the hospital room. "She's the most beautiful baby and you're the most beautiful mom."

"Marie!" Jane called from the kitchen rousing Marie from her dream. "Supper is ready. We should get done before the doctor arrives."

Marie was awake now and thought of Bobbie's birth. *Rick said that Bobbie was a beautiful baby, too, but we were scared about how to take care of him.*

"Marie!" came Jane's voice again. Marie rolled out of bed and made sure Rick was covered. She touched his forehead again. It was cold.

A gentle "I love you, Rick" ended Marie's reminiscing.

Chapter 8

DR. WILLARD

Dinner was goulash. Jane knew how to cook a nice marinara sauce with noodles. Bobbie had eaten a Chips Ahoy chocolate chip cookie before supper and still had chocolate on his face. Marie smiled at her family and Sarah, who sat around the table waiting for her. They were all just about to have desert (more cookies) when the knock came on the door.

Dr. Willard was of medium height and weight with silver hair and a kind face.

"Please come in. Can I take your coat? Thank you so much for coming," Marie said as she opened the door for him.

The doctor kept his coat on. The house was about 52 degrees.

Sarah jumped up and ran to the doctor giving him a big hug. "I'm so glad to see you."

"Yes, it's been too long. How is your mom doing?"

"She's good. Deb's dad needs you."

Marie interrupted, "Dr. Willard, my husband is upstairs in bed. He hasn't responded to anything for over 36 hours."

The doctor nodded. "Let's go up and see him." Turning to Sarah, he said, "Do you have your team talking to the Creator and the Light?"

"Yes, Doctor Jim."

Bobbie began following the doctor and Marie toward the stairs. They both stopped while Marie observed Dr. Willard face everyone. She knew that Bobbie wanted to go to be with his daddy. Deb stood her ground like a soldier, but Marie perceived that her battle was in her heart and mind. Love tangled with hate; forgiveness with perceived justice. Sarah seemed expectant with a pensive stare exhibited by pursed lips. Poor Jane just held a forced smile. Marie understood that Jane just wanted her family to be fixed and didn't know what to do to make that happen. She presumed that Dr. Willard saw the same things she did in her family.

The kind doctor looked at Bobbie, but spoke to everyone. "Wait down here while I check on your dad with your mom. I'll let you know when you can see him."

Deb immediately went into her role of being a second mom to Bobbie. She took his hand and said, "Come on Bobbie. You made a mess at the table. Dad would like a clean table when he wakes up." Bobbie reluctantly went with his sister with some protest.

Sarah whispered to Jane, "Deb is really good with Bobbie."

Jane replied, "Yes, she is."

Dr. Willard and Marie went upstairs. Dr. Willard had two battery-operated lamps with him. Candles were used downstairs.

The doctor felt Rick's skin, listened to his breathing, took his blood pressure, and took his pulse. He opened Rick's eyelids to look into his eyes. Dr. Willard said, "I believe your husband has hypothermia. He also could have suffered a mini stroke or TIA. It is good that this room hasn't warmed up quickly. I'll need to call the Beckerville Ambulance Company. They can keep the ambulance cool enough to transport Rick to the hospital. Marie, go down and ask the older woman to get the children into your living room and find an activity to do. The medics will need a clear path to move Rick on the gurney."

Marie ran down the stairs and spoke to Jane. Hope surged inside her for the first time in hours.

"Jane, take everyone into the living room. Perhaps you could tell stories. We need a path for the medics who will be coming on an ambulance."

It only took a few minutes for everyone to gather in the living room. Bobbie sat on Nana's lap in the recliner. Deb sat on the couch. Sarah sat on the opposite side of the couch from Deb.

Sarah stood up and asked Jane, "Can I read from the book that talks about the Light to you, Deb, and Bobbie?"

"That would be nice, Sarah."

While Marie was downstairs, Dr. Willard made the call. "Ron, we have another hypothermia case. He looks to be about 40, so he should have a good chance of survival. There may have been a TIA, so, we have to be very careful moving him, but he needs to be in the hospital for recovery. Do you know if the hospital is taking any more cases?"

"The hospital has been refusing cases for about three days now because about twenty-five percent of the people with these symptoms have developed a physical problem. Some have died. The hospital can't have that statistic in their records."

"That's what I was afraid of. People are being left to die. The house I'm in is quite cold, especially this bedroom. It is, I'd say, about 50 degrees. We may have to make this a hospital room. Could you bring over a couple of generators, a pump for intravenous administration of salt water which we can warm, bags of salt water, and catheters. I may put some warmed salt water into his abdominal cavity, and I'll need a catheter for urine. Also, I'll need a couple tanks of humidified oxygen with a face mask to apply oxygen to warm the airways. And, I'll need help in changing this patient's sheets. "

"I can provide these things, but will have to report the need to replace them."

"Put them on my tab. That is why I called you."

"Yeah, I know. I'll get Jack to come with me to help, and I'll bring two generators. See you in about twenty minutes."

"Thanks." Dr. Willard then bowed his head and started talking.

Marie walked in and saw Dr. Willard with his head bowed.

"Dr. Willard, what are you doing?"

"I'm talking to the Creator in the name of the Light. I'm asking for healing for Rick and for your family."

"What about Rick? Can't you do something now?"

"Marie, we have to wait for two friends from Beckerville Ambulance. They will help me make this room into a hospital room instead of transferring Rick to the hospital. The hospital can't take any more of these hyperthermia cases. It is important to talk to the Light and ask for healing. Would you like to join me?"

"I believe this Light exists because I've seen His hand, but I also see ice and I don't understand how to get this Light or the Creator to heal Rick or get rid of the ice."

"You can't demand what you want or do anything on your own power. The ice is the buildup of unforgiven things in a person's life. The Light comes from the Creator. He became a man so He could take all the gray, murky ice away from every person and put it on Himself. That ice brings death. So, the Light died with all that ice on Him. However, since He lived a perfect life and the ice wasn't really of his making, He didn't stay dead. And because He took that terrible ice from us, we, too, can be judged by God as perfect and can live again with the Light after we die. Until then, our life in this world will be filled with hope, love, joy, and peace no matter what trials we face. Marie, you just have to tell the Creator that you believe in the Light and ask Him to forgive you for the things that created the ice in your life. After that, ask Him to heal Rick."

"I believe that and did that even though I don't understand completely. But right now, can't we do something for Rick? How are you going to change this drafty old room into a hospital room?"

"Do you have a clothes dryer?"

"Yes, but no electricity."

"Gather some blankets. One of the men is bringing an extra generator. We'll be able to warm the blankets in the dryer."

Marie's hope began to diminish. There were other cases like Rick's. Thoughts about Howard saying Rick hadn't worked for him for a year plummeted Marie's mind. The call from Jacobs's

Grocery also crossed her mind. Could her experience with the blue light and Dr. Willard's words be the answer to her feeling of hopelessness? Marie prayed: "Light, I believe in you. If you bring hope, I could use some now."

Marie went downstairs, gathered two blankets and put them in the laundry room. She glanced into the candle-lit living room where Sarah was reading from a book.

Sarah read, "The people living in darkness have seen a great light; on those living in the land of the shadow of death a light has dawned—Matt. 4:16."

"Dark outside," piped up Bobbie.

Sarah continued, "The darkness is really that gray ice that you see."

"Mommy sees ice. Debbie sees ice. Bobbie don't see ice," responded Bobbie. Everyone gasped in surprise. Bobbie really had no idea of the situation everyone else was in.

Jane said, "We learned about the Light as children and heard talks about Him at funerals, but we didn't think of Him in everyday living until my Lee had a stroke. I know somehow that the Light is the answer to getting rid of this surreal ice."

Marie walked into the room. "Dr. Willard said that you have to talk to the Creator in the name of the Light and ask for forgiveness for holding onto hatred and ignoring the Creator. The ice is from us, Jane. Dr. Willard said that it is the result of everything we do or think which is bad or wrong. He said that the Light took all that ice on Himself and died even though He was perfect so we could be thought of as perfect by the Creator and be free of the ice." Everyone starred at Marie.

Deb stood up quickly and stomped towards her room. As she passed Marie, she said, "I thought you would tell us about Dad, not this Light stuff."

Jane must have seen the disappointment on Marie's face and grabbed her daughter-in-law's hand. "Let's talk to the Creator." Sarah came over and put her arms around both women.

Bobbie jumped up between them saying, "Me too, me too."

Marie began: "Please, Creator, forgive me for all the hate and judgment in my life. Help me to understand. Please heal Rick and Deb. In the name of the Light."

Jane continued, "Please forgive me, too. Please heal Rick and Deb and be with Lee in the name of the Light."

Jane hugged Sarah and went to check on Deb while Marie returned to her bedroom upstairs. Deb didn't respond to Jane's knocking on her bedroom door.

Jane looked around the living room. The ice was no longer on the windows or the walls. A blue light filtered into the kitchen and living room even though it was dark outside.

Marie somehow felt peace replacing anxiety. As she entered her bedroom, she heard Jane singing.

"Thank you, thank you."

The ice was gone in the bedroom. "Dr. Willard, the ice is gone!"

The good doctor looked up at Marie and said, "I'm so happy for you. Rick probably still sees ice in his mind. Several people are talking to the Creator about him. We do need to keep this room cool and only gradually warm it. Do you have a clean set of bed sheets?"

"Yes. They're right here in the closet." Marie went into her walk-in closet where she kept extra bedding.

Downstairs Sarah was knocking on Deb's door. Jane joined Sarah in the knocking.

Jane called, "Deb, come out and see."

Deb came to the door and opened it. "See what?"

"The ice is gone!"

Deb looked into the living room. "The ice is still there, Grandma. You're getting crazy like mom and Bobbie"

Bobbie claimed, "I not crazy!"

Deb gave Bobbie a slight smile and said, "I want to be left alone."

Just then the ambulance arrived.

Chapter 9

THE HOSPITAL ROOM

When the ambulance arrived, Marie opened the door before Ron and a second man with him, Jack, knocked. They were carrying the things Dr. Willard had asked them to bring.

Jane was unable to keep anyone in the living room. Deb came out of her room; Bobbie's eyes were wide open. He tried to follow Ron up the stairs.

Deb ran and grabbed Bobbie's arm. "No, Bobbie."

Bobbie cried.

Jane said, "Deb, I'll take Bobbie into the living room, but I need you to get one of his books and read to him."

Deb did as Jane had asked, though she mumbled about it. Sarah sat quietly down on the couch.

Jack asked, "Where is your dryer? I'll hook it up to the generator so we can warm blankets." Marie showed him the laundry room and he quickly connected the dryer to the generator, threw in a couple blankets, and said to her, "Let's go see Rick." They ascended the stairs.

Marie stepped back as Jack joined Ron and the doctor by Rick's side. Dr. Willard began giving orders. "Marie, while we change the sheets, would you go grab the warmed blankets."

Marie expected the blankets to take about 15 minutes to warm, but agreed. She ran downstairs and, to her surprise, found one blanket was already warm. The men put an IV in Rick's arm that did not hold Teddy. They fastened a blood pressure cuff on the other arm. Catheters went into his abdomen. Two pumps ran with warm salt water. Another catheter released urine and an oxygen mask covered Rick's nose and mouth. Rick looked like he was in the hospital. The warm blanket went on Rick's body.

"Marie," asked Dr. Willard, "could you find more blankets and put them in the dryer? We'll change out three for three about every 30 minutes."

Marie went downstairs to recheck her children's rooms for blankets. *How am I going to get more blankets and keep everyone warm?*

The phone rang. "Hello."

"Marie, is everything alright? I see an ambulance in your driveway, and it has been there for a while."

"Ruth, thank you for calling. We have two medics and a doctor taking care of Rick. You wouldn't have a couple of blankets I could borrow, would you?"

"Rick is really that ill! I'm so sorry. I'll bring five blankets over right now. Howard may grumble, but I love your family and feel so sorry about yesterday morning."

"Thanks." Marie didn't have time to ask about why Howard fired Rick.

Ruth came over a few minutes later. She handed Marie five blankets and said, "I don't know what you're going through, but I want to help. Call if you need anything." She turned to leave.

Marie put three of Ruth's blankets in the dryer and took one warm blanket upstairs. The room seemed brighter. Dr. Willard was still talking to the Creator. Ron and Jack seemed to be doing the same thing. She joined them.

During the next several hours and through the night Rick's temperature gradually rose. By morning, Rick's eyes fluttered open.

Even though Dr. Willard had been up all night, he didn't seem tired. He asked Rick, "Are you ready to get rid of the ice?"

Will Rick understand this when he's barely conscious?

Rick's eyes were glazed over, but he glanced around the room and said, "I want … to forgive … and be … forgiven."

Dr. Willard took a few moments to tell Rick about the Light and lead him in a talk to the Creator asking for forgiveness and stating his belief in the Light. Blue Light touched Rick. The doctor, with Ron and Jack's help, removed all the equipment that was attached to Rick.

The three men turned to Marie. Dr. Willard said, "We can take Rick to St. Matthew's now if there is room. It will take time for him to recover, and we don't know the effects of a TIA if there was one as yet." Dr. Willard called the center.

Marie went downstairs to make coffee for everyone. She had lost all sense of time. Sarah had phoned her mom and Sally was now sitting asleep with her daughter on the couch in the living room. Jane held Bobbie, both of them sound asleep in the recliner.

Where was Deb? Marie checked her room. She lay motionless and cold. With more strength than Marie thought she had, she dragged Deb upstairs to Dr. Willard.

He shook her awake.

"Young lady, you need to have hope. You are special and loved and so is everyone else. Don't fill your heart with bitterness. The Creator gave you a gift. You know how to care for your brother. He needs you. Your mom needs you and your dad needs you."

Rick heard them from his bed. He whispered, "Deb … I … love you." Tears ran down Rick's face.

Deb went to her dad. She looked conflicted. "Your eyes don't freeze," was all she could say.

Ron and Jack had gone to the ambulance to get a stretcher, and returned just then.

Dr. Willard looked at both the men. "The hospital rehab center is full, but the hospital has a teaching program for residents with a few rehab rooms which may have an opening." The doctor made the call and then hung up with a smile on his face. "Let's go."

The men carefully lifted Rick's body onto the stretcher and covered him with two blankets, strapping them on.

Dr. Willard said to Marie, "You and Deb can ride in my car. I'll drop you off at the hospital."

Deb complained, "Why do I have to go?"

"Your dad needs you," the doctor replied.

Marie and Deb followed Ron and Jack downstairs and watched them put Rick in the ambulance.

Everyone was awake now. Jane looked exhausted.

Sally said, "I can stay and help out until noon so Jane can get some rest."

Marie walked outside with Deb and Dr. Willard. The ambulance was gone. The sun was out. Their Maple tree branch was no longer on the Ford Escape SUV. The snow sparkled with diamonds.

Dr. Willard said, "The ice is gone for you, Marie. Don't ever turn away from the Light. Why don't you drive to the hospital in your car? That way, you'll be able to drive home without hiring a cab."

"Okay, doctor. Thank you for everything."

Dr. Willard drove away.

Marie reached into her purse and found the keys. "Let's go, Deb."

"Mom, can't you see the tree branch on the roof of our car? Don't you remember trying to pull it off?

Marie unlocked the door. "Get in, Deb."

Deb crawled over the driver's seat and sat on the passenger seat. "This car won't go, Mom, and you're crazy to try."

Marie started the car, drove out of the driveway, and headed for the hospital.

Deb stared at her mom. "Be careful, Mom, the frozen branch is still on the top of the car."

Chapter 10

THE TEACHING REHAB CENTER

A mountain of paperwork overwhelmed Marie as she registered Rick for rehabilitation. She wasn't sure how much of the cost insurance would cover. The only way Marie could keep Rick at the center until insurance was applied was to promise to pay at least $200 a week until the bill was paid. She had no idea how long rehab would be.

Please, Light. Please, Creator, help. Please, please help.

Marie and Deb were allowed to see Rick for a few minutes and then asked to come back during visiting hours which were 6-8 PM. Marie spent those moments talking to her husband. "Rick, I love you. I'm sorry for all the burdens I put on you. Everything will be okay."

Deb said nothing.

After seeing Rick, they were led to an administrative waiting room in order to conference with a social worker.

Deb asked, "How are you going to give them $200 a week?"

"I don't know, but I know things will work out even if changes have to be made."

"What changes? I'm not going back to school."

The social worker invited Marie into her office. She spoke to Deb. "Honey, you can watch TV in the waiting room while I talk to your mom."

"Great."

Marie followed the social worker. The social worker smiled as she graciously motioned for Marie to sit down. "Mrs. Winton, I am Rebecca Fitzgerald. My job is to help you and your family adjust to the rehabilitation needed by your husband. We have contacted your husband's employers and they faxed insurance information to us so that we can help you with insurance decisions. It appears that Mr. Winton lost a job with Handson Construction a year ago, but kept paying the premiums for the insurance in a deal between Handson Construction and Jacobs's Grocery where Rick has worked for this last year. Mr. Winton reported other income as an independent contractor, but took out no additional coverage. The insurance from Jacobs's Grocery is good for the balance of this month, but will expire on the first of next month unless a new agreement is made. I can show you various insurance options and what programs may help you."

"Jacobs's Grocery?" Marie questioned.

"Yes. Evidently, they lose a lot of employees because the owner is a bit gruff. Mr. Jacobs attached a note to the records saying that he expects a spouse or relative to take an employee's place if that employee leaves without a two-week notice or insurance will be automatically cancelled."

"That's unfair."

"Unfortunately, your husband signed the contract."

"I've never worked at a grocery store. I was a teacher's aide before I had Bobbie."

"Before we deal with health insurance, let's fill out this form about your family so we can determine what programs may help you. How many children do you have, and what are their ages?"

"I have two children. Deb is twelve and Bobbie is four."

"Are you employed?"

"I am a stay-at-home mom. I homeschool Deb and take care of Bobbie who has Down Syndrome."

"Are you aware that the State has programs for Downs children?"

"I wanted to raise him myself."

"The State can help, but you will need to be looking for work or be employed. There is a program for displaced homemakers which helps women find employment when their husbands are no longer able to provide for the family."

"Deb refuses to go to school. She suffered teasing there." *She needs me, too.*

"We can conference with the school counselor to help Deb adjust. Give me a few minutes and I'll check on what teaching aide positions there are in the districts around us."

An awkward silence ensued in which Marie again prayed in her mind. *Creator, I put my trust in You. Please help in the name of the Light.* The presence of the Light seemed to calm Marie's anxiety.

"There doesn't seem to be any aide positions available presently except at the Becker School for special children. The pay is less than the public school, but it would qualify you for State assisted health insurance based on income."

Rebecca figured out finances with the grocery job compared to the aide job and insurance premiums. "Wow, you actually come out ahead with the aide job and State insurance because the State insurance covers 80% of the cost here for rehab. But, when rehab is done, the grocery store job would be slightly better."

Marie nearly jumped out of her seat. "Thank you Light!"

Rebecca's eyebrows raised causing furrowed lines on her forehead. "Are you okay, Mrs. Winton?"

"I've been to the Becker School. May I call them?"

"Sure. You can use this phone. I'll put in the number. While you make the call, I'll bring up a list of local job opportunities."

Marie made the call. "Hello, Meagan?"

"Yes, this is Meagan. Can I help you?"

"This is Marie Winton. I visited there with my daughter, Deb, yesterday."

"Of course, I remember."

"I understand that there is an opening for an aide at your school. I do have experience as an aide at a public school and with taking care of my son. If I was an aide at the school, could I bring Bobbie with me? Could he go to your school?"

"Marie, I'd love to interview you. Some of our children spend part of their day with us and part at the public school. We also have helpers who work with the children in their homes in order to give parents a break or cover care when the parents are working. If you work for us, your son would be charged half tuition which is often partially covered by the state. There would still be some costs."

"May I ask how this opening for an aide happened?"

"It takes a special person to deal with the children. You will need training. Some children can get violent. Roger is great with them, but we need another person to work with Roger in special cases. The person who left couldn't handle the job."

"I'll fill out an application, Meagan."

"Wonderful. I look forward to seeing you."

Marie hung up the phone and told Rebecca, "I want to fill out an application for the Becker School and for the State insurance. I'll also fill one out for the grocery store. Is it possible to have two insurance policies so that the rehab would be covered in full?"

Rebecca responded, "I don't think you need two policies. You should hold onto the one with Jacobs's Grocery until you are approved for the State insurance if that is your choice. Some companies offer supplemental coverage, especially for catastrophic circumstances. The trick is to find one that offers help with pre-existing conditions. I'll give you information about two of these companies and how to reach them. And, Marie, don't worry about the $200 requested at registration. You do have insurance unless Jacobs's Grocery cancels it before the end of the month. Take some time to decide about insurance this week. Make some calls and contact me about questions or help with application forms. You have enough to handle with your family right now."

"Thank you, Rebecca." *Thank you, Light.*

"It's my job to help. So, call and make an appointment as often as you need. Now, getting back to employment, it is best to send out a few applications for possible jobs. You might be surprised at what you may be qualified for."

"Where do I get the forms?"

"They are online. I can help you with the applications you mentioned. Here is a printed-out list of local jobs and local agencies that may be of help along with their contact information. All aid from social agencies is based on monthly income, so, you won't be able to apply for aid from these until you have a month of pay receipts. Let's get started on those two applications for employment."

The women finished the two applications. Rebecca informed Marie, "You will be called for an interview if an employer is interested. I'm sure something will come up. Now we need to talk about registering Deb for school. She needs as close to a normal schedule as possible while you deal with work, insurance, your husband, and your four-year-old. I suggest that we make an appointment with the school's counselor and principle at the Beckerville Middle School today. Deb won't have to start for a few days, but everything can be planned so Deb and the school will have time to deal with anticipated changes."

Marie understood that she couldn't work and homeschool, so, she agreed to let Rebecca make the call. *Everything is happening too quickly. Deb won't like this, but what can I do?*

Rebecca made the call. "Hello. This is Rebecca Jones. I am a social worker at the hospital and there is a twelve-year-old girl whose father is in rehab here. I need to see about setting up an appointment for her and her mom to talk about registering for classes. She has currently been homeschooled."

An appointment was made for that afternoon with the vice-principal and the school counselor. Marie left Rebecca's office thanking her and dreading Deb's reaction to the news.

Marie sat next to her daughter and touched her shoulder. "Deb, let's go home for a while. After lunch we'll need to go to an appointment at the middle school."

Deb stood, threw up her hands, and screamed, "I knew it! You're giving up on me! I don't matter to you! Only Bobbie matters!"

Rebecca came out of her office. Her face was blank as she stared at Deb.

Deb scowled at her. "What are you looking at?"

Deb crumbled back onto the couch, curled up in a ball, and pushed Marie away.

Marie did not see the ice covering her, but she knew it was there.

"Deb, before we go home, we are going to visit the Becker School for Disabled Children."

Rebecca still stood outside her office. Marie surmised that Rebecca was confused and surprised with her reaction to Deb's outburst.

"So now you think I'm disabled!" Deb shouted.

"No. I need to talk to Roger. Come on, Deb. You can't stay here." Deb begrudgingly followed Marie to the car.

Chapter 11

RETURN TO THE BECKER SCHOOL

When Marie and Deb entered the foyer of the Becker School, Meagan waved at them from her office and immediately went to greet them. "Rebecca called to say you were coming."

"Is Roger available?" Marie asked.

"Actually, he is on break right now. I'll call him. Please, sit down while you wait."

Deb and Marie sat down on the same sage green sofa they had sat on the day before. *So much has changed in a day.*

Roger seemed overjoyed to see Marie and Deb again. *Does he treat everyone this way?*

"Roger, it is good to see you again. I have a question which I hoped you might answer for me."

"Okay."

"Did you ever hate anyone?"

Deb stared at her mom.

Roger sat down in the chair next to Deb. "I hated my mom and dad. They were sad when I was born. My aunt took care of me. My sister had everything. I had nothing. My hate made me angry. Are you angry?"

Surprised, Deb said, "Of course!"

"Angry isn't good. It hurts you. Moms and dads don't hate. Sometimes, they don't know how to help their kids."

Deb said, "My mom knows how to help Bobbie. Dad works all the time and only hugs Bobbie. I don't matter."

Roger looked at Marie. "You and your mom came here to see me."

"My mom asked for you. I didn't." Deb's belligerent eyes stared at her mom.

"Deb, I love you so much. I homeschooled you so that you didn't have to deal with the teasing. We didn't have the money for many things you wanted to do. I saw how good you were with your brother that I began to depend on you for help. Maybe if you go to school, you will be able to join some clubs or play an instrument."

Frozen tears clung to the corners of Deb's eyes.

Marie's tears flowed down her cheeks.

Roger pulled a small silver heart from his pocket. "My aunt gave me this. When it's not in my pocket, it gets cold. When I rub it or keep it close in my pocket, it is warm." Roger then gave it to Deb. "Keep your heart warm."

Roger then got up, shook both of their hands, and returned to the office.

Meagan had been watching from the office. She came out, now drying tears from her cheeks. She knew this was about Deb, so, she didn't speak to Marie about the job. She spoke to Deb. "We have a program matching high school students who take child development with some of our children who attend the public school part-time. I think you would be a good candidate for that program. You are special."

Deb said, "I know. And loved."

Marie glimpsed a miniscule amount of gentleness return to Deb's face. It would take time. *Light, please help my daughter see the love around her.*

Marie could sense that Megan cared about Deb. As they prepared to leave, Marie thought, *I hope that I get this job. Meagan and Roger must be wonderful to work with.*

Deb seemed distraught and remained silent as they headed home, but she kept the heart in her pocket.

Chapter 12

HOUSEHOLD CHANGES

Deb and Marie arrived home before noon. On the way home, Deb stared out the car window. The security in Deb's life had been stripped away and her emotions were like a roller coaster. Silence seemed to be best for now. When they pulled into the driveway, Marie said, "I'm so glad you came with me today."

"It didn't make much difference, Mom."

Jane met them at the door. "I can't wait to hear how everything went."

Bobbie hadn't run to the door to greet his sister and mom. He was playing with Sarah and Sally in the living room. Deb went to her room without saying hello to anyone.

"Jane, everything will be all right. The social worker at the hospital helped me apply for a job at the Becker School, the grocery store, and for State aid. I have one week to figure out health insurance. There are other jobs to apply for, and Debbie will have to go to the middle school. If I work at the Becker School, Bobbie's tuition is half and the State may help with the remainder."

Sally, Sarah, and Bobbie had heard Deb go to her room. Sally and Sarah were now standing in the kitchen. Bobbie stood in front of Deb's door and was pounding on it.

"Debbie! Debbie! Come out. Come out. Don't you like me?"

Deb didn't answer.

Marie picked Bobbie up and hugged him. Tears were running down his face. "Bobbie, Deb loves you. She is sad about Daddy and school. She needs some rest."

"Bobbie sad, too."

Sally spoke to Marie, "Marie, I have to go to work, but I gave Jane my number. If there is anything I can do to help, please call."

"Thank you, Sally, and thank you, Sarah."

"Mrs. Winton," Sarah said, "I can help show Deb around school if she'll let me."

"That's very kind of you, Sarah. I have an afternoon appointment for Deb at the middle school today."

Jane helped Sally and Sarah gather their things. As they opened the door to leave, Sarah turned and handed Jane the book she had brought. "This will help Deb, even if only you read it and talk to the Light for her."

Jane smiled and gave Sarah a hug. "Thank you, Sarah."

"Bye," they all echoed.

After the door shut, Jane turned to her daughter-in-law. "Marie, you're going to need help. I can stay today, but then I need to get back home to take care of Lee. Our neighbor has been helping out with Lee while I've been here. However, I can give you a day every week to help clean and fix a meal. That way Bobbie can have spaghetti and chocolate chip cookies."

Bobbie piped up, "Don't want a cookie, want Debbie."

The two women and Bobbie went to Deb's door and knocked. Jane spoke first. "Deb, could you help me figure out how to help your mom? You know so much about taking care of Bobbie and about taking care of the house."

There was no answer.

Marie tried to reach out to her daughter. "Deb, I'm sorry I put so much responsibility on you. I promise that when I start working, you will not be given more."

Deb responded in a sobbing voice, "That's not true. You'll need me to help more, or you'll have Sarah and her mom over here doing my jobs and I'll be left out."

Bobbie was crying, too, and again knocked on Deb's door. "Love you, Debbie."

Deb opened her door and Bobbie gave Deb a huge hug.

Marie watched her two children embracing each other. Crying seemed to be as common the last couple of days as breathing. "Deb, Bobbie, you will always be brother and sister. No one can destroy that."

As Marie gazed into Deb's room, she noticed that some of the gray ice clung stubbornly to corners. *If the Light has come into our lives, why do I see the ice again? Does it have something to do with Deb and not me?*

Jane spoke, "Marie, we had better get lunch together if you are going to make those afternoon appointments. By the way, the electricity came back on."

"What? When? You're kidding! Does the thermostat work?"

"All the rooms but Deb's have heat. I also called Kelly's Repair and told them that you really needed the stove fixed."

"Jane, we don't have the money."

"I charged it on my account. Now don't complain. You can pay me back when you do have money. I'm not worried. I know where you live."

"Jane!"

"Not a word."

Bobbie piped up, "Want a cookie."

Jane responded, "After you eat a sandwich."

Jane made peanut butter and jelly sandwiches while Deb reluctantly perused her closet wondering what would be best to wear to school. Bobbie stood by her offering help.

"Me like red," Bobbie stated.

Deb said, "I like blue."

Marie heard them and suggested purple, a mixture of red and blue. Deb didn't have anything purple, but she did have a nice cranberry blouse that looked great with jeans. They all agreed.

Bobbie wanted to go to school, too, and ran into his room to choose school clothes. "Bobbie," Deb told him, "you're not going to school today."

Jane called, "Lunch is ready. Let's eat."

Bobbie brought his red shirt to the table determined to go to school with his sister. The family settled around the table for a few minutes of peace. Bobbie's red shirt went on the back of Jane's chair for later. Jane then asked, "Marie, this has been on my heart all morning. Is Rick able to have visitors?"

"Yes, Jane. The visiting hours are 6 to 8 PM, but we may not be able to be with him that whole time. You certainly can come with us and we can take turns seeing Rick and taking care of Bobbie. Bobbie won't be allowed to see Rick."

Deb said, "Nana, I can take care of Bobbie here at home. You and mom should go to see Daddy."

Jane gave Deb a bear hug. "Thank you, sweetheart. I'm going to make your mom stop at Jacobs's Grocery on the way home from the middle school so I can buy your favorite ice cream. It's Moose Tracks. Right?"

Bobbie heard ice cream and exclaimed, "Chocolate."

"Any flavor is okay," Deb said, "but you don't have to buy anything."

"Moose Tracks and chocolate it is."

As Deb and Marie got ready to leave, Jane whispered to Bobbie. "Bobbie, you can wear your red shirt when we have chocolate ice cream tonight."

Chocolate stains on a red shirt. Oh, well, it will make him happy.

Chapter 13

BECKERVILLE MIDDLE SCHOOL

Silence again filled the car's atmosphere on the drive to the Beckerville Middle School. Marie was nervous. Deb fiddled with her fingers and occasionally ran them through her hair.

The secretary at the front office had worked at the elementary school where Marie had been an aide. "Marie, it's been a long time. How are you?"

"Fine, Donna. It is good to see you again. My daughter and I have an appointment with the school counselor at 1:45 and the vice-principal at 2:15."

"Yes, I see that on the schedule. I'll give her a call and tell her that you are here. Her name is Julie Harris. She is one of our school counselors. We also are fortunate to have a school psychologist as part of the counseling team for families going through hard times."

Donna made the call. "Julie, Mrs. Winton and Deb Winton are here for their appointment."

Donna turned toward Marie and said, "I'll take you down to the counselor's office in five minutes. You can have a seat here while you wait."

The five minutes seemed like five hours. Deb couldn't sit still, crossing and uncrossing her legs. *I want to flee from this place, probably as much as Deb.*

Donna motioned their way. "Follow me. Julie's office is at the end of hall B. When you are done, come back to the main office." Donna knocked on the closed door.

Julie opened it and invited Deb and Marie in. "It is nice to meet you Deb. It's nice to meet you, Mrs. Winton. Please have a seat."

After settling into the cushioned chairs, Julie shared, "I have Deb's file up to fifth grade plus the reports you have turned into the school from Liberty Home School Association. So, Deb should fit in well in the second half of seventh grade. It will take a little time to adjust to the classes, but we are here to help. From the reports, Deb, you have done exceptionally well academically. Do you know any students here?"

"Why can't I just teach myself at home?"

"An adult must be in the home in order to meet the state requirements for homeschooling. Based on your homeschool record, I'm sure you could teach yourself many things. There are also activities here which you don't have at home. I'll show you a list of our courses and other opportunities."

Julie pulled out a list of courses, intramurals, clubs, sport teams, and musical groups. She laid it down in front of Deb and then asked again, "Do you know anyone who goes to this school?"

Marie responded, "Mrs. Harris, my husband is in rehab at the hospital. This is a sudden circumstance that we have to deal with. It is changing our lives. Could we just make up her schedule and then see if there is a student with the same schedule whom you would recommend?"

Deb remained silent as she perused the list. "What classes do I have to take?"

"English 7, Algebra, Global Studies, Science 7, a language, and an elective. I see you have been taking Spanish. I would recommend the second semester of Spanish I. Then you can choose an elective and a gym which are every other day, making six classes a day."

Deb glanced at Marie with exploring eyes. Marie felt like her daughter was being thrown into a culture she didn't understand and didn't want to join.

Deb made the course choices. "Child Development for an elective. Swimming II for gym."

No one smiled, but Julie said, "Those are good choices. I know someone who has those classes who can show you around. You may even become friends. Her name is Sarah McCain."

Deb screamed, "NO!!!" She jumped to her feet and stalked out of the office.

Marie excused herself and opened the door to the hall. Julie followed her. Deb stood in the hall encased in a garment of surreal, murky ice. Julie likely didn't see it and probably didn't understand Marie's outburst.

Why do I still see ice?

Marie grabbed her daughter's shoulders. "Deb, Deb, look at me. The Light is real. Don't let hate take your life." Marie gathered her daughter in her arms to warm her and show her love.

Deb snuggled in, and looked at her mom. "I'll try for one day."

"You are very courageous."

Mrs. Harris stared at them. "Mrs. Winton, I'll email these forms to Principal Miller along with a report on our meeting. I'm sure he can go over them with you." Mrs. Harris closed the door to her office.

Marie and Deb slowly found their way to the main office and again sat down waiting for the appointment with the vice-principal. *I'm sure Mrs. Harris's report isn't positive.* The office staff simply ignored the Wintons. Donna notified them when Mr. Miller was ready to see them. His office was connected to the main office.

A boisterous, "Hello," startled both Marie and Deb as the vice-principal opened his door and invited them in.

"Mrs. Winton and Deb, I am so glad to meet you. I'm Don Miller. About six years ago, your husband made a beautiful shelf unit for my home. My wife thinks it is the best piece of furniture that we own. I heard about Rick being taken to the hospital rehab unit. I'm so sorry. We will help in any way we can here at school."

"How did you know about Rick?"

"The social worker from the hospital called to make the appointments and explained the situation. My son, Alan, is also in a group of teens who have been praying for your husband to recover." Mr. Miller genuinely seemed concerned when he stated, "You must be exhausted!"

A bold question came from Marie's heart. "Do you believe in the Light, Mr. Miller?"

"Alan has tried to tell me about this Light person or thing, but I'm not ready to trust in anything I can't see or understand. I will, however, respect your faith. Now let's get to the reason for our meeting. Mrs. Harris contacted me and gave me a course schedule for Deb."

Marie noticed a little covering of ice on Mr. Miller's book case. *Why am I seeing this ice? Will I ever be rid of it?* Marie felt that she had to ask: "Have you heard of any other families who have had cases of hypothermia?"

"It is some kind of virus which some families have had to deal with. Now let's get back to Deb."

Mr. Miller looked over the schedule and directed his conversation now to Deb. "Mrs. Harris thinks it would be best if Mrs. Green, our Special Ed teacher, shows you where all your classes are located. The Becker School also called requesting that Deb be considered for the program we have each Monday morning. During first period, teens are matched with special needs elementary children to help these children adjust to their school environment. Deb, Mrs. Green could meet with you on Monday morning, interview you, and then show you around the school. "

Deb sat motionless saying nothing.

Mr. Miller spoke with compassion in his voice. "My wife, Michelle, had the Hypothermia last year. That's when Alan started talking to this Light thing or person. Michelle got better, but she walks with a limp now. I do hope Rick gets well. It was hard on us. So, I understand some of what you are going through. Deb, you don't have to come to school until Monday. That will give you time to look over the books or syllabuses for your classes. I will ask the teachers to get the materials ready for tomorrow morning. Mrs. Winton, could you possibly pick them up after 9:30 tomorrow?"

"Of course. And I'm sorry you had to deal with the ice."

"What ice?" asked the principal.

"The gray ice that reminds us of the wrongs we have done."

"The virus causes some graying and cracking of the skin and it is cold, but it is not ice. Alan has spoken of the same crazy idea. It's one thing to talk to a deity. It is another thing to hallucinate. I'm sorry, but you do need to reframe from talking about the ice you see. You already had an outburst in front of Mrs. Harris. We can't have demonstrations of your hallucinations in school or you may face explaining them to Child Protective Services. Do you understand?"

Deb was about to say something, but Marie touched her hand to quiet her and spoke calmly to Mr. Miller even though she could see ice developing on his suit coat. "Yes, I understand. Thank you for your time, Mr. Miller. Also, thank you for the kind words about my husband. I will be here tomorrow about 10:00 to pick up the material for Deb."

Mr. Miller put on his welcoming façade and escorted Marie and Deb to the door. "It was a pleasure to meet you both. I look forward to having Deb as a student here. If we can be of any help, let us know."

"Thank you, Mr. Miller."

Marie turned to Donna. "Donna, I'll be here tomorrow to pick up materials for Deb. Have a nice day."

Donna acknowledged the statement. The Wintons left the school solemn and silent.

When Marie reached the car, Deb said to her, "Mom, I can't go here."

Chapter 14

BACK TO THE P&R COFFEE SHOP

"Mom, why are we stopping here again?"

Marie parked the car and told Deb that they needed information. Deb begrudgingly followed her into the coffee shop. Grayed ice remained on the façade of the building. Sally was waiting on a table, so they sat down waiting for her to come over.

"Marie, Deb, how is it going today?"

"We just had a meeting with Mr. Miller at the middle school. He told us that we are not allowed to talk about the Light. I was warned that Child Protective Services could be called if I mentioned the surreal ice."

"Wow! That's ridiculous. Mrs. Miller was in almost the same shape as Rick last year. Sarah invited their son Alan to her teen group and he started talking to the Light and learning about the Creator. Alan began to see the surreal ice on his mom, and when he talked to the Light, the ice started to disappear. Mrs. Miller also put her trust in the Light. However, she didn't fully recover. Mr. Miller believes that his wife had a virus and gets very angry at Alan for his faith. However, Alan is allowed to come to the teen group as long as he doesn't mention the ice or miraculous healing. Mr. Miller is determined not to trust in anything but science. He can be a nice man, though."

Deb interrupted, "How can you say he is nice when he threatened to take Bobbie and I away from our parents! He is right about one thing. My mom and you and Sarah are a little crazy about this Light Person."

"Hey, waitress, are you going to wait on us or just go on gabbing?" shouted a man from a table near the window. Sally had to continue to work.

"Mom, if we sit here, we'll have to order something."

Deb was right. They couldn't stay.

Another man at the corner table was watching Marie and Deb. He was the same man who was there the first time they had come into the coffee shop.

Is he here all the time?

He made a gesture as if inviting them to join him. Marie started moving toward him when Deb grabbed her arm. "Mom, are you crazy?"

In spite of her feelings, Deb followed Marie to his table. Ice covered him. He warmed himself with coffee. His eyes were penetrating blue surrounded by blood-shed white. His disheveled hair was a mixture of gray and black. There was a handsome man under the depression that clung to him like an incurable illness.

"Ladies, please sit down." They sat down across from him.

"How is Rick, Mrs. Winton?"

"Please, call me Marie. Rick is in rehab at the hospital."

"You paid for my coffee yesterday. Folks don't do that for me. I want to buy you coffee and the young lady a hot chocolate. Maybe you'll have time to talk to Sally, then."

Marie tried to refuse his offer, but he called Sally over to give her the order.

How could this man who was so mean yesterday be so kind today?

"Sally, get a good cup of coffee for Marie and a hot chocolate with whipped cream for the girl and put it on my tab."

"Got it, Carl," Sally said as she handed in the order and picked up an order for another table.

"Mrs. Winton.... Marie, could you tell Rick that I miss him?"

"Of course. When he is able to see more visitors, I'll let Sally know and she can tell you."

"Oh, I can't go there. Just tell Rick."

Sally brought the drinks over. Marie added cream and sugar and sipped her coffee. *There is something about Carl that makes me want to know more about him. However, now is not the time to ask questions.*

Carl looked at Deb and showed compassion. He had overheard the conversation about Mr. Miller and said, "I didn't like school either. Your dad always talked about how mature and smart you were."

"Why did my dad talk to you?"

"We had the same troubles. I have to go now." Carl got up and left them at his table while he exited the building.

Customers thinned out in the next few minutes and Sally came over. "I don't know how you are both able to keep going. You both need rest."

"I'll try to sleep after seeing Rick tonight. Deb is watching Bobbie while Jane and I go to the hospital." Marie pursed her lips together while she stirred her coffee. "Sally, I don't understand. How can people be covered with the surreal ice because of wrongs they have done and be considerate, too? How do I relate to them? How can I be myself and not hurt the feelings of others or be hurt by them?"

"Marie, our Creator loves every single person because He created each one. He allows some of us to see this gray unnatural ice which negatively impacts our own lives and leads us to seek the Light. Some of us see this ice in other peoples' lives. God wants us to look beyond that to see the hurting person imprisoned by it. You have just begun to seek and trust in the Light and you have had to deal with many trials. Don't let the frozen wrongs in other peoples' lives bother you right now. Just ask our Creator to show them the Light. Carl and Mr. Miller are lost in darkness with broken hearts. The Light wants to heal them. Maybe the Light will use you to touch their hearts."

"I have one more question, Sally."

"Yes?"

"Why is ice covering the façade of the coffee shop?"

"I haven't thought about that for quite a while. Many people come here with problems. The apartments upstairs are low-income flats and the tenants frequently come and go. There is ice on the outside, but you will notice that there is no ice on the inside walls."

Marie glanced around. It was true. Gray murky ice may cling to a customer, yet the inside of the coffee shop was free of it.

Sally continued. “The owner, cook, and I have talked to the Creator and asked that this place be a refuge for troubled souls. That’s why even though I get worried about finances, I continue to work here. By the way, the ‘P’ in our name stands for peace and the ‘R’ stands for rest.”

Deb responded, “We don’t need to be around troubled souls, Mom. Let’s go. Remember, we’ve got to stop for ice cream before going home. And I’m tired.”

Marie thanked Sally and mulled over Sally’s words as she and Deb returned to their parked car and headed to Jacobs’s Grocery.

Chapter 15

FAMILY PREP FOR REHAB VISIT

After quickly picking up the ice cream at Jacobs's Grocery, Deb and Marie drove home. Bobbie was waiting expectantly already wearing his red shirt. He had also helped Jane prepare more peanut butter and jelly sandwiches for supper.

"Ice cream!" Bobbie shouted as they entered their home.

Deb was holding the ice cream high over her head as she spoke to Bobbie. "First, I get a hug and a sandwich."

Bobbie was quick to give his sister a hug, but seemed disappointed that sandwiches were a priority over ice cream. At least they were peanut butter and jelly.

Jane assured them that the sandwiches were well made. "Bobbie was in charge of the jelly and I did the peanut butter. It was a team effort," she announced.

Jane gave Bobbie a high-five before continuing. "It took a little bit of cleaning up, but that was fun, too. And, Marie, I added a little honey to your sandwich."

"Honey!" exclaimed Deb with a grimace on her face.

"Deb, your mom and I agree that honey is good on almost everything. Besides, we need a little sugar to keep us going, and honey is the best sugar I know of."

Bobbie was already eating his sandwich before the rest of the family even began.

"Bobbie," Marie said to get his attention, "slow down and remember, you have to drink your milk, too, before ice cream."

Marie couldn't believe what Bobbie did next. He rolled his eyes just like his sister.

Deb started laughing. She then rolled her eyes just the same way while looking at Bobbie. That began a rolling eyes contest around the table.

Soon everyone was ready for ice cream. This was something everyone could enjoy together.

At 5:20, it was time to get ready for the evening visit to the hospital. Jane made two thermoses of coffee. Marie got Bobbie ready for bed while Deb changed.

Deb said, "Mom, I think that I'll get in bed with Bobbie and read him a story. We'll probably be asleep when you get back. Say hi to Dad." She then whispered to her mother, "Check on Teddy, too. Bobbie will miss sleeping with him."

Bobbie already had an armful of books for Debbie to read.

After goodnights, hugs, and kisses, Jane and Marie got in the car and headed for the hospital. Jane had been holding everything inside, but now silent tears ran down her face.

"Are you okay, Jane?"

"Rick is my son. I've seen him grow up as a curious, compassionate child. He always loved people and having fun. He poured himself into sports and fixing things just like his dad. You and the kids were the only thing that could draw him away from those activities. But I didn't teach him about the Light. Sports filled our Sundays. We were fine without the Light until tragedy came. Rick's high school coach got killed in a car accident caused by a drunken teen just after Deb was born."

"I remember. Rick was devastated. He kept saying, 'How could God allow that to happen?' and, 'That kid should be put away for the rest of his life.'

"Lee had similar comments. The funeral didn't draw them closer to God. They judged God instead. But the coach's wife, Mary, believed that her husband was in heaven because he believed in the Light, and she forgave the teen. That's when I started to attend church services occasionally on Sunday, just to try to understand life and stop the growing bitterness in my son and husband."

Marie's eyes became watery now, too. "Rick is a great dad, but the last few years, he has grown more distant. It's my fault."

"No, Marie, it's not. Rick loves you so much. I have come to realize that peace and joy in life really come from a relationship with the Light. I just feel so guilty for not teaching Rick this truth and for all the mistakes I've made as his mom. I can't do anything to change the past, and I'm so scared for Rick, Marie. I know you are, too. You have been so brave."

"I'm not brave. You are a wonderful mom. I couldn't have gone through these last couple of days without you. We need the Light. I felt His love and peace when I saw His hand and the Blue Light."

"Blue Light?"

"Yes, when I was upstairs alone with Rick and trying to talk to the Light, a Blue Light appeared with a hand reaching out to me. It was the Light, Jane. I know it was."

"I believe you. After Lee's stoke, he felt defeated. He did little except for watching television. One day, he saw a woman singing hymns at a televised crusade. The woman was in a wheelchair. She was happy, too. Lee started to change back to his old self, but different. Joy now came from watching Christian programs instead of working on cars or playing sports. About a month ago, he said that he believed that the Light would remove all the ugly ice from our lives. Marie, we need the Light. I'll talk to Him now if you like for both of us and Rick."

"Of course. Please talk to Him."

"Light, I heard in a sermon that You never leave us or forsake us. Please forgive us for all our mistakes and failures. Please be with us now. Heal Rick and help him to really know You."

Jane and Marie remained quiet for the rest of the ride to the hospital. Even though Blue Light did not fill the car, a special presence, which they both felt, calmed their fears.

Chapter 16

REHAB VISIT

After parking the car in the garage and noting what floor they were on, Jane and Marie found their way to the rehab training center. Marie saw patches of ice everywhere. It even clung to the information counter.

Why did this ice cling to inanimate objects when it was created by peoples' bad choices? An employee from behind the counter asked, "Can I help you?"

"We came to see Rick Winton."

"Only one visitor at a time. Dr. Willard is with Mr. Winton currently and will be finished soon."

Jane and Marie stared at each other wondering why Dr. Willard was here during visiting hours. Jane had brought the book about the Light which Sarah had given her. She opened it up to the book of John.

"Marie, you won't believe this. This is right at the beginning of this book of John. 'In the beginning was the Word, and the Word was with God, and the Word was God. He was with God in the beginning. Through him all things were made; without him nothing was made that has been made. In him was life, and that life was the light of all mankind. The light shines in the darkness, and the darkness has not overcome it.'

Marie, that ugly cold surreal ice is part of the darkness and the Light has already overcome it. The Light can heal Rick! He created Rick's life. The Light is God and is with God. I don't understand it, but I believe it."

Just then, Dr. Willard entered the waiting area. The women were overjoyed to see him and expectant for good news.

"Dr. Willard, it is so good to see you. How is Rick?" asked Marie.

"It is good to see you, as well. Rick slips in and out of consciousness. His bloodwork is improving. We won't know if the TIA caused any damage until Rick gains full consciousness. I'm not registered as his doctor. He is under the care of the rehab doctor, Dr. Stevens. However, I can read his charts and can visit during visiting hours."

Something bothered Marie about Dr. Willard's countenance. "What's wrong, doctor?" she asked.

"It's none of your concern. I'll continue to check in on Rick and a couple of my other patients for as long as I am allowed to see them. Let me know if Rick responds to your visit. The Light be with you." Dr. Willard smiled as he left.

Jane patted Marie's arm. "Marie, you visit first and I'll go after you."

Marie approached the woman at the information counter. "May I see Rick Winton now, and how long am I allowed to be with him?"

"It is recommended that you don't stay more than 15 minutes. However, since Dr. Willard visited and there are two of you, I suggest you take just 5 minutes each. As Mr. Winton improves, we can increase the visit time. I'll take you to his room. Have a nice visit."

IVs were connected to Rick's arms and he was connected to a heart monitor. "Rick, it's me," Marie said as she gently touched Rick's hand, then his forehead, and tenderly leaned forward to kiss his cheek. Rick felt warmer now.

Where is Teddy? Marie's eyes searched the room, but Teddy was nowhere to be seen. Rick seemed to be sleeping. The quiet five minutes flew. "You're going to be okay, Rick. You're going to be okay." *I'll find out about Bobbie's precious Teddy.* "Jane's here to see you. I'm so glad you called her. I'm here, too, and always will be.'"

Marie believed that his eyes fluttered open and closed as he softly muttered her name.

"You are the best husband and father, Rick. I wouldn't want anyone else. The Light is going to heal you and give you back to us." Marie fought back tears.

Rick softly voiced the strangest thing—"Light, Light"—just like Bobbie had said it many hours before. It was not said in despair, but in confident hope like words in worship.

Marie told Rick about the peanut butter and jelly sandwiches and ice cream. She told him that his mom promised to make spaghetti once a week for them and that his dad was doing well. Finally, Marie said, "Everyone is asking the Light to heal you." When the five minutes were up, Marie kissed Rick again and left him with, "I love you."

Jane had been reading the book of John in the waiting room. She seemed to be full of joy. "Marie, there is so much in here about the Light. I'll share it with you later." The same employee escorted Jane to Rick's room.

When the employee returned, Marie went up to the counter and asked, "Excuse me, could you tell me your name?"

"Rita."

"Rita, when my husband was brought in, he had a teddy bear with him. Do you know where that teddy bear is now?"

"Every patient has a bag with personal items they bring in with them. We store them for two days until they are picked up and then we toss them to keep things sanitary. I'll check in our store room. Just wait for a couple of minutes."

Oh, Light, please give us Teddy back. I think it is just as important to Rick as it is to Bobbie.

Rita returned with a bag marked Rick Winton. His clothes and Teddy were in the bag. "Thank You, Light."

Rita asked, "Did you say something?"

"I just thanked the Light, that is God, for giving Teddy back to us. Our four-year-old boy with Downs slipped it under his daddy's arm to make his daddy better. In a strange way, it did seem to make Rick better."

Rita responded with her own story. "I have a preemie here in the Neonatal ICU. I've put a recording of my voice and a teddy in her isolette. I know how to sterilize a stuffed animal under hospital rules. I could do that for you. Everyone in this unit needs support. If a teddy bear can give support, then why not? I'll also do my best to keep it away from Dr. Stevens's rounds. He is a little strict."

"I couldn't ask you to do that for me. You must have so much to handle right now. Congratulations on the birth of your baby. How old is she?"

"I definitely want to do this for you. You are the first person who has congratulated me on the birth of my child. I had her at 26 weeks gestation. She is 2 pounds, 8 ounces and beautiful." With frozen tears, Rita continued, "I go to see her twice a day and bring her breast milk. There is time between my work and the trips to sterilize Teddy. I'm so scared that she may have cerebral palsy. She had a minor brain bleed yesterday."

Even though it was probably against hospital rules, Marie went around the counter and gave Rita a sympathetic hug. They were united as moms in a very special way. Marie wrote her phone number on a card and handed it to Rita. "Call me if you need someone to talk to."

"Thank you, Mrs. Winton. I'll put Teddy under Rick's arm as soon as it is sterilized. I'm sure it will be here tomorrow evening." Rita put Teddy in another special bag. The rest of Rick's things would go home with Marie.

Another visitor entered the waiting room.

Jane soon returned with a smile on her face.

"What happened, Jane?"

"I read John 8:12 to Rick. It says, 'When Jesus spoke again to the people, He said, "I am the light of the world. Whoever follows me will never walk in darkness, but will have the Light of life."' The Light will give Rick life. The Light is Jesus. In my old age, I am beginning to understand some of the things I learned as a child. Perhaps the Light will give me another chance to tell my son about His love."

"Did Rick respond to you?"

"I was holding his hand in mine and he gently squeezed my hand."

Rita smiled at these two women and said, "Goodnight, ladies. I'll see you tomorrow."

Hope filled their hearts as they left the rehab center. Marie took Jane home so she could be with Lee and then drove to her home looking forward to seeing her children and sleep.

Chapter 17

NIGHT DREAMS

Deb had fallen asleep with Bobbie in his bed. Books were scattered on the floor. Marie quietly picked up the books and made sure both children were covered with the comforter. She had almost forgotten about the danger of the ice. Bobbie's room seemed to be free of it.

Marie peered into Deb's room. *I wonder if I'll see ice in there?* Frost framed Deb's bedroom window. Gray ice encased the legs of Deb's bed, dresser, and desk. Rick was not the only one struggling for life.

Although Marie did not want to go into her bedroom alone, she was so exhausted that she had to sleep. After climbing the stairs, Marie checked out her bedroom. *Will there be ice here, too*? What met her eyes was like a miracle. Only a little frost sparkled on both windows. *Is it because I told the Light that I was sorry for being a selfish grumbler? Is it because I talked to Him or because I reached out to His Hand?* Questions mingled with anxious thoughts about Deb, hope for Rick, and wonder about all the people she had met that day. *What will tomorrow bring*? Marie did not want to contemplate what the future might hold. She just needed to sleep. She crawled into bed without setting any alarm.

Fear of Deb going to Beckerville Middle School grabbed Marie's imagination in her first dream.

Deb was dressed in her cranberry blouse and nice jeans. She met Mrs. Harris as soon as she entered the school.

Mrs. Harris questioned Deb. "Does your mother have emotional outbursts that upset you?"

"Only when she is really tired or sees ice on us."

"How often does she see this surreal ice?"

"It's only been for the last couple of days."

"Since your dad's illness?"

"Yeah. Why all these questions?"

"We want to make sure that you and your brother have a stable home life."

"It is stable."

"Why were you so upset about Sarah McCain showing you to your classes?"

"Hey, I didn't come to school to be interrogated!"

"I am making an appointment for you with our school psychologist for today at 2:00. Your teacher will be notified. I've contacted the State Department of Child Welfare with Mr. Miller's consent to interview your mother at your home as soon as possible."

"You can't do that! You are a beast and I won't come here to school!"

With that, Deb tried to walk out of the building. The police officer was called and Deb was taken to the police station. Child Welfare was notified. Marie was told to come to the station immediately.

In Marie's dream, she was working at Jacobs's Grocery stocking the ice cream aisle. Mr. Jacobs picked up the call from the police station. "Mrs. Winton has to finish her shift here before going anywhere, "he said.

"Was that call for me?"

"The police have your wayward daughter at the police station. They want you to go there now, but if you leave, you'll be fired."

Marie left anyway because Deb needed her. When she arrived at the station, Mrs. Harris escorted her into a room with Deb and several adults.

"Mom, these people are demented. They think that I need a psychologist and that you are crazy!"

Surreal ice covered everyone in the room and rose to the ceiling on every wall. Marie wanted to run to Deb, embrace her, and leave. "Deb, you are a smart, mature, intelligent girl. I love you so much."

Marie asked the group of adults, "Why did you bring Deb here?"

"Mrs. Harris has filled us in on your emotional outburst at school. Mr. Miller has also shared that you hallucinate about seeing a strange kind of ice on people and things. We understand that this may be a passing reaction to your husband's illness, however, children should not suffer because of your break down."

"I am not having a breakdown. I have a job and my mother-in-law is watching my son while I work. I visit my husband once a day at the rehab center. We have friends and support."

A robust woman named Pamala confronted Marie. "Mrs. Winton, it is our concern that both your children are in a high-stress situation. We are making a recommendation for them to be put into foster care as soon as homes are available. Your home and your situation will be evaluated monthly. When we feel it is safe to return your children to you, we will notify you."

"You can't take my children from me. You can't! Please Light, help!

Marie's pleas woke her up. Sweat dripped from her forehead. She quietly slipped downstairs to look in on her children. They were still safe in bed sleeping. Marie slowly climbed back upstairs and crawled again into bed. Thank you, Light, that that was just a dream. Please keep my family together.

Again, Marie drifted into sleep and dreamt. She was drowning in a lake and could not break through the surface because sheets of grayed ice enclosed her in the body of water. She was trapped fighting for her life.

Help! Help! Marie's cries coursed through her mind. No one could hear a scream even if she could make one. She heard chopping. People were chipping away at the ice. Finally, after long moments, they broke through and pulled Marie out. Sally and Sarah were there along with Dr. Willard and Ron and Jack, the two EMTs. Megan and Roger from the Becker School for Disabled Children stood beside Jane and Rita. Lee was there in his wheelchair, too. A couple of people who were unrecognizable because of mist from the water stood on the shore.

There was also a figure clothed in Blue Light with His hand reaching out to Marie. Suddenly, all the ice melted and Marie stood on lush green grass alone with the figure. He spoke to her."

"You don't have to see the surreal ice anymore because you know it is there. It is not of my making. All people have turned away from Me and my Father to go their own way. Each one builds up that surreal ice in their lives, but it can be removed and a new life can begin. I took all that ice, all those bad decisions, all those hurts and guilt on myself and died a terrible death on a Roman Cross to pay the price for those wrongs and to remove that clinging ice forever. Don't waver in believing in me, Marie, no matter what happens in your life. I gave my life for you and will always be with you."

Marie fell on her knees at the figure's feet and lifted her hands to Him. He touched her hands, smiled, and disappeared.

Sleep now came to Marie without dreams until the sun woke her up in the morning.

Chapter 18

FACING THE DAY

The clock read 9:00 in the morning when Marie woke. Sunlight was streaming through the window. Deb and Bobbie were laughing downstairs. Instead of getting dressed, Marie threw on a robe and slippers and went downstairs. "So, what are you laughing at?"

"We made pancakes, Mom. Bobbie helped," replied Deb.

Bobbie was covered with flour and was drawing in the flour that had spilled onto the table.

Marie had to laugh, too. "Are there any pancakes for me?"

Bobbie stopped drawing and proudly handed his mom a pancake. Deb gave her a plate to put it on.

"This is a real treat! May I have two?"

Bobbie handed his mom two more pancakes.

After they cleaned up, Marie told Deb, "Honey, I have to go to the middle school to pick up the materials they gathered for you. I also want to stop at the Becker School to see about a job there. Could you watch Bobbie while I'm gone?"

"You can pick up the materials, but I'm not going to that school. If you have to work while Dad is getting better, I'll take care of Bobbie. You still can homeschool me when you are home." Marie's first dream caused anxious thoughts to hamper the otherwise special morning.

How can I send Deb to that school? Will they try to take my children from me?

"I'll consider every possibility for your education, Deb. I will have to work at least 40 hours per week and find a way to take care of Bobbie, too. Whatever we decide, it may be temporary until your dad gets better. I love you very much. I am also talking to the Light about school."

Deb rolled her eyes and Bobbie imitated her. Then Deb defiantly stated, "Don't depend too much on the Light. Dad isn't better yet."

Bobbie tried to imitate his sister's expression and said, "Light, Light."

It appeared to Marie that Deb was stubbornly trying to hold herself together. She couldn't surrender the little control she had. However, Marie didn't see any ice on her, and when she glanced into Deb's room, there was no surreal ice there either. A shiver went down Marie's spine. *Was my second dream real? What about the first one?*

Marie arrived at the middle school about 10:30. but didn't go in before talking to the Light. *Please, Light guard my words and actions so I don't bring any harm to my family.*

Donna was at the reception desk. "Hello again, Marie. I believe all the materials Deb needs are here."

"Thank you, Donna. I'm sorry that I didn't ask you about your family yesterday. Is everyone doing well?"

"Matt and I separated last year. John is in his first year at Beckerville Community College and Jenny is a junior in high school."

"I'm sorry about you and Matt."

"It's for the best, believe me. Here is your bundle of class material for Deb."

Mr. Miller came out of his office and asked, "Do you have a few minutes, Mrs. Winton?"

"Yes." Marie whispered the Light's Name, *Jesus*. The first thing she noticed was that no surreal ice clung anywhere in the office or on Mr. Miller.

"Please take a seat, Mrs. Winton. Mrs. Harris has suggested that Deb see the school psychologist to help her through this rough family time. You will need to fill out a permission form."

"May I meet the school psychologist first to answer questions concerning Deb and to be able to give Deb more information about the professional she will be having a session with?"

"We prefer to see the child without parental influence so we can determine the child's state of mind and emotional issues."

"I see. May I take the form with me and think about it?"

"We need to get this scheduled as soon as possible in order to give Deb a smooth transition from homeschooling into the public school program. I will let you take the form with you, but please bring it back on Monday."

"Thank you, Mr. Miller." Marie rose from the chair determined not to send Deb to this school, but she only had a couple of days to figure out what to do. *Why, Light, is this happening?*

The Becker School appointment was next at 11:30. Megan invited Marie into her small office. The walls were painted a light blue that seemed to change to green or almost white depending on how the sunlight coming through the picture window reflected off surfaces. A gray tweed rug covered the floor. Two overstuffed gray-blue chairs faced Megan's desk which took up one-third of the room. Files of neatly stacked papers sat on the left side of the desk. A large book, notepad, and phone rested on the right side.

Megan took her seat in a high-backed computer chair behind the desk. Marie sunk into the comfortable chair nearest the window. One whole wall opposite the window held posted pictures of children and verses from the book about the Light. A verse hung on the wall behind Megan. Marie's eyes and heart were drawn to this quote handwritten on parchment paper in a simple golden frame. "The Lord is my Light and my Salvation; Whom shall I fear? The Lord is the Stronghold of my life; of whom shall I be afraid? Psalm 27:1"

Could the Light really take away the fear that welled up inside of me? Still, there is a special peace in this room.

Megan interrupted Marie's thoughts. "Marie, I have been looking into ways we may help you out. The job here as an aide is for 30 hours a week. It is minimum wage, but we do have a special pre-school which Bobbie can be in while you work. Fees are based on income with up to 25% being covered by the state. As an employee, you get 50% off the fee. There are also other state programs for disabled children which could cover the other 25%. I think you would be a good fit for the aide position, and I believe with these programs, Bobbie can attend here for free."

Marie smiled and cried at the same time. Megan allowed Marie time to compose herself before responding. “Megan, I can’t thank you enough. The job sounds like a perfect fit.”

“Marie, you have been through a lot. I am a good listener and want you to be at peace here while you work. If there are burdens you can’t handle, it will affect your performance. The children here will need your full attention.”

“Megan, I just left the middle school. They want Deb to see a school psychologist and won’t let me have any influence on the meeting. Deb refuses to go there, and I am so afraid that they want to take my children from me. I am a good mom and I do want this job.”

“Did they give you a form to sign?”

“Yes, it’s here. I couldn’t sign it.”

“That’s good. You are not the first family to be given this form. We have psychologists who work with some of our children and their families. There is one whom I think will be best for Deb and you. The school may demand that Deb see a psychologist, but they would have to accept an approved private psychologist’s treatment in place of the school psychologist.”

“Won’t that cost money?”

“It again can be funded by a state program. Excuse me while I make a call in the room next door.” A small office adjacent to the room they were in contained more files, a small desk, and a landline phone similar to the one on Megan’s desk. Megan closed the door.

While Marie waited, she talked to the Light and read more verses on Megan’s office wall. Psalm 34:17 seemed to jump into her anxious heart. “The righteous cry out, and the Lord hears them; He delivers them from all their troubles.”

Thank you, Light. Please give me strength and take away the anxiety.

When Megan returned, she noticed that Marie's raised tense shoulders had relaxed.

"Marie, Dr. Michael Hill is willing to help out. He said that he can see Deb tomorrow at 3:00. You can go with her. He will determine if he needs to ask Deb some questions without you present after meeting with both of you. Michael is a believer in the Light and attends the same church I attend. He is a nice man and also has a wonderful therapy dog. He won't charge you for the first visit to give you time to deal with the changes in your life. I'll help you with the state forms we need for you and Bobbie here. Michael will talk to you about the school form."

"I don't know how to thank you."

"Take the job."

"I certainly will. Rebecca from the social service department at the hospital informed me that you provide health insurance."

"We have a policy, but you may need to look at other options as it is minimal. You may qualify for a federal policy. I can call the agency after we fill out employment forms." Megan helped Marie with all the forms for work and applications for state programs.

"Marie, I would like you to start a week from Monday. That will give us time to process the paperwork. Could you come in next week sometime to get an idea of your responsibilities and meet the rest of the staff?"

"Sure. How about Tuesday at 9:00?"

"That will be fine."

Roger came into the office just as they finished talking. He reached out to Marie's hand and said, "Let's talk to the Light."

Megan smiled. "Roger has a special sense of peoples' needs." Megan, Roger, and Marie joined hands as Meagan prayed. "Father, Creator, Light, thank you for sending Marie, Deb, and Bobbie here. You know all things. Please bring peace, wisdom, and the knowledge of your will to this family. Show both Deb and Marie what they need to do concerning Deb's education. Bring healing to Mr. Winton and let them all know and understand how much You love them in the Name of the Light. Amen."

Megan's prayer gave Marie the courage to stop at Jacobs's Grocery before going home. *Maybe I could convince Mr. Jacobs to keep Rick's health insurance going until the federal insurance takes over.*

In the parking lot, Marie recognized the EMTs, Ron and Jack, who had helped Dr. Willard with Rick. They were walking into the store. She ran toward them shouting, "Ron, Jack!"

Both men turned around and were at first confused about a middle-aged woman running toward them. Jack spoke first: "Mrs. Winton?"

"Yes. You were both in my dream last night, but I don't know why. The Light was there, too, and Dr. Willard."

The three of them moved away from the entrance while Marie told them about her second dream.

Ron thought for a moment. "Maybe there is a reason why you met us here."

"I was just going to see if Mr. Jacobs would hold onto Rick's health insurance until I can get federal coverage. I need it to keep Rick at the rehab center."

Jack and Ron both smiled. "We know why you met us here. Mr. Jacobs is Jack's uncle. We will go with you to talk to him." They entered the store together.

Ron knocked on Mr. Jacobs's office door. Jack greeted his uncle. "Hey, Uncle Ben, how are things going? I brought a couple of friends with me. Can we come in?"

Even though Marie couldn't see any ice anymore, she felt its presence. This was a cold room. Even the walls were a yellowed beige. A gray metal desk with a scattering of papers and pens seemed to be shoved into a corner with one plastic black chair behind the desk.

"Jack, you know I am busy. I had another employee quit this morning and that Rick Winton got sick. It will probably make the health insurance premium go up. Fortunately, I can take them both off the policy on Saturday. What do you and your friends want?"

"Mom's birthday party is tonight at 5:00. We came to invite you and pick up some things for the party."

"She probably wants 10% off."

"No. She just wants you to come."

"What are you having for dinner?"

"Delmonico steaks, fries, garden salad, and of course chocolate telegram cake and vanilla ice cream."

"Well, I will try to break free. Is that all?"

"Uncle Ben, you know my friend, Ron, and this is Mrs. Winton, Rick's wife."

Mr. Jacobs tried to hide behind his desk as he diverted his eyes away from Marie. "Mrs. Winton, you must realize that I have a business to run."

Strength that wasn't her own helped Marie to respond. "Mr. Jacobs, I understand. But, one thing I don't understand. Why did you call me the day my husband got sick and demand that I come to work when I didn't even have a job here?"

Jack spoke to his uncle. "Are you doing that old trick again; trying to demand spouses to take over shifts when their husband or wife either quit or are ill?"

"The insurance is expensive, and I need people here to run the registers and stock the shelves."

Marie spoke calmly to Mr. Jacobs. "I could work on Saturday. I have a job during the week, but need some more money. Would you keep the insurance going until I can get a federal policy?"

Jack said, "Yes, he will keep the policy going whether you work here or not. Uncle Ben needs to make some concessions for a better reputation and to be able to keep his employees. Uncle Ben, make the call now to the insurance company to keep Mr. Winton's policy, and I'll put an ad in the paper that you are hiring and that employees will get 10% off their groceries bought here."

"You can't tell me what to do, Jack."

"My dad does own some stock in this store. I love you Uncle Ben, but sometimes you hold onto money too tightly, and it not only hurts others, it hurts you and your business."

"Okay, Okay!" With that said, Mr. Jacobs made the call.

Marie sincerely responded to all that had transpired in the conversation between Jack and his uncle. "Thank you, Mr. Jacobs. I would like to start working for you on Saturdays starting a week from this Saturday because you have been so kind as to keep Rick's insurance. I could also use the 10% off groceries."

"A week from Saturday!" was Mr. Jacobs reply, but Jack broke in with a smile.

"Mrs. Winton needs to set up arrangements for her children. You wouldn't want her to bring them to work with her. You'll see, uncle, kindness brings results. Jack gave his uncle a hug. "See you tonight at 5:00."

Ron and Marie shook Mr. Jacobs's hand. Mr. Jacobs glumly accepted the situation.

This is a man who needs prayer. He must be encased in ice.

Marie thanked Ron, Jack, and the Light before heading back to the car. *Only God could put this all together.* New hope surged through Marie's veins. *Who else was in my dream?*

Bobbie and Deb were happy to see their mom arrive home. Deb was ready for a break from Bobbie.

"How did it go?" Marie asked.

"I've read every book Bobbie has twice. We did an exercise video and ate some more ice cream. I think Bobbie needs a nap so I can have one, too."

Bobbie added. "Me make sanwich."

"Oh, yeah, Mom, we had more peanut butter and jelly."

"I promise not to have that for supper. Deb, why don't you rest for a while, too. I will get Bobbie to take a nap and we'll talk when you get up. I have a couple of phone calls to make."

Deb didn't argue.

Bobbie exclaimed, "No nap."

"Yes, Bobbie, a nap. I'll get you cleaned up and play a song for you on your CD player."

"I want Teddy."

"You gave Teddy to daddy for his nap, remember?"

"Wake up Daddy, wake up Daddy?"

"Daddy needs a long nap. He loves Teddy, too. How about sleeping with Brian, your lion?"

"Okay."

Marie got Bobbie ready and he fell asleep as soon as the CD started.

Marie called Jane.

Lee answered, "Hello."

"Lee, is Jane home?"

"She has a doctor's appointment today for her legs. That woman of mine doesn't stop. What's up?"

"Jane said that she could give us one day a week to help out. I'll be starting to work on Saturdays a week from this Saturday and was wondering if that would work for both of you. I feel awful asking."

Lee hesitated and said, "Marie, if you brought both Deb and Bobbie here, Jane and I could watch them on most Saturdays. That way, Jane won't be trying to clean your house as well as cooking meals and watching Bobbie. I get worried about her being on her feet so much. Actually, we do have some good news that may help you out, too."

"What is that?"

"Rick's brother and his family are moving back here from Virginia. Kevin got a job at the hospital as an emergency room doctor and his wife, Sophia, will be substitute teaching in the Beckerville City School District. They just closed on a house. They wanted to move to be closer to us after my heart attack."

"That's wonderful." *Kevin and Sophia and their children never visited us much in the past, and Sophia seemed nervous around Bobbie. Is this good news or another challenge?*

"Kevin wants to help with Rick, too. He also likes to fix things and can help out at your home. Their kids are both in elementary school. Joe is 8 and Marci is 10 now. Perhaps the cousins can play together on Saturdays and Sophia can help, too."

"That sounds good, Lee. I won't work forever on Saturdays at Jacobs's Grocery … just until Rick can work again."

"Marie, you are not a burden. We love you, Deb, and Bobbie. Besides, I need to be needed, too. I would love to read to Bobbie."

"Thank you, Lee."

"Of course. I'll have Jane call when she gets back. Bye now."

"Bye." *Why was I felling discouraged? The Light was putting so much together in miraculous ways.*

The next call was to the Baptist Christian School in town to ask about tuition. Marie knew it was a long shot, but at least she could ask. She made the call.

"Union Baptist Christian School, can I help you?"

"I am calling to ask about tuition for the second semester of seventh grade and if you have an opening for a student."

"The tuition for half a year would be $4,000 plus supplies. There is room. May I ask, is this Sally McCain?"

"No, I am Marie Winton." *Why did they ask if I was Sally?*

"Oh, I am so sorry. Sally called earlier and asked the same question. Is there a problem going on?"

"Yes. We believe in the Light and want our children out of the public school."

"The Light? Do you mean Jesus?"

"Yes.

"Our school does give preference to families who attend the Baptist Church. Our members already give some support to those in attendance. What church do you attend?"

"I haven't joined one yet. I have homeschooled my daughter with Liberty Christian Academy resources."

"I have heard about their material. Can I help you with anything else?

"No, thank you."

Light, I don't know what to do about Deb. Please guide me. After I see Rick this evening, I must call Sally to ask her why she called the Baptist school.

There was a knock on the door. Marie opened the door. "Ruth, oh, I'm sorry. I haven't washed the blankets you loaned me yet."

"Don't worry about that. I'll take them dirty and wash them myself. You have enough to do. Marie, I want you to know that Howard fired Rick a year ago. We actually had an argument over it. Rick's work wasn't up to par according to Howard. I said that you folks needed help. Howard said that we couldn't help by watching your children. Howard is bitter about us not being able to have children. He said that every family should take care of their own business. I was so mad at my husband. I love kids and taught at the Montessori school until it closed seven years ago. Today, I put my foot down and told Howard that I was going to come over here and volunteer to help you out if you could use me. I hate just staying at home, cleaning, and cooking."

Marie hugged Ruth for the first time in four years and sensed that they would become close friends. *Ruth may not know the Light yet, but she is close to His compassion.*

"Ruth, I have about an hour before I have to get supper. Do you have time? I'll fill you in on what is happening." Marie spent the next hour sharing everything that had transpired in the last couple of days. Ruth had a hard time understanding the ice, the Blue Light, and Marie's new faith in the Light, but she understood the trauma and was very concerned about Deb.

"Marie, let me check into homeschooling rules. There are a few other teachers who worked at the Montessori school who might be interested in helping Deb while Rick is in rehab so she can continue her homeschooling. Perhaps working with teachers other than you will help her transition to a public or Christian school as she gets older."

"Oh, Ruth, I am so grateful, and I'll find some way to pay you eventually if you can work this out." Ruth and Marie hugged each other again. They were neighbors and women sympathetically sharing personal struggles.

As Ruth opened the door to leave, she gasped. "Marie, I see ice on my house! It is gray and Howard is inside. I have to go check on him." Ruth grabbed the blankets and started making her way toward her frozen home as quickly as she could.

"Call me, Ruth, and let me know if Howard is okay."

Please, Light, reveal Yourself to Ruth and Howard in a way that they can know you are real, and help them to trust in You. Show Ruth how to help Deb if that is your plan.

Chapter 19

RUTH AND HOWARD

Ruth wondered: *How did these yards freeze in just the hour I was visiting Marie?*

The cold handle on the front door burned Ruth's bare hand as she opened it. Sandy barked a joyous greeting.

Howard shouted, "It took you long enough."

Howard sat in his usual spot on the right side of the flowered couch with his feet resting on a unique, carved maple coffee table. The surreal ice covered Howard from his white buzz haircut to his stocking feet. Ruth gasped, "Howard, are you alright!?"

"What's wrong with you, woman? I'm not sick. It's Rick that has problems. By the way, how is Rick?" Howard took his light brown eyes off the TV and looked at his wife. "Ruth, you look like you saw a ghost. What's wrong?" Howard got up and walked toward Ruth.

Ruth backed away.

Howard firmly stated again, "What's wrong!?"

Almost whimpering, Ruth replied, "Howard, you're covered with ice. The gray ice is real, Howard. You are in danger."

"I knew it! You have spent too much time with Marie. You are not allowed to go over there anymore."

"Howard, you can't tell me what I can and can't do."

"Be reasonable, Ruth. Use your teacher's head. Marie is hallucinating. It's been reported that some people hallucinate about this ice. I'm going to call Dr. Clark's after hours number right now." Howard made the call.

"Dr. Clark's emergency line."

Ruth heard her husband explain the reason for his call.

"This is Howard Stanton. My wife, Ruth, is a patient of Dr. Clark's. She just came home from visiting our neighbor who hallucinates about seeing weird ice. Now my wife says that she sees the ice, too."

"Mr. Stanton, Dr. Clark does not deal with psychological problems. He can see Ruth if you wish and give her a referral. There are some excellent psychologists in our medical group."

"My wife isn't crazy! She just has been spending too much time with our neighbor." Howard hung up.

Ruth decided not to talk about the ice with anyone except Marie. She also decided to appease her husband in order to gain peace. She had been doing this for years. Although she felt lonely, at least she had a place to live, her books, and her precious dog, Sandy. Ruth loved her husband, but they lived separate lives only engaging in superficial conversation at supper. Howard watched TV and Ruth read books. Ruth began her plan of appeasement. "Howard, I'm sorry that I scared you. I'll put these blankets in the washer and then, why don't we go out for supper?"

"Wow, Ruth, that was a unique way to get me to take you out to dinner by pretending to see murky ice. You really had me worried. I called the doctor. How are you going to explain my call at your next visit?"

"I'll tell them that I needed to get your attention so you would take me to dinner."

Howard smiled. "Well, it worked. Where do you want to go?"

"I've heard about this little coffee shop not far from here called the P&R coffee shop. They serve sandwiches and desserts and are not expensive."

"Where did you hear about it? Isn't that the place with low-income apartments above it?"

"Yes, that's the place. I must have read about it or heard someone mention it. It is a small business in our community, and I'm curious. If it is good and inexpensive, we may be able to go there once in a while and tell our friends about it. My Montessori friends would like to go out to lunch occasionally, and we need an inexpensive place to meet." Ruth felt guilty deceiving her husband; however, she felt it was the only way to protect herself and keep their marriage peaceful.

Howard accepted his wife's explanation. "Let's go. I'll warm up the car. Come out in five minutes."

"Thank you so much, Howard. You are thoughtful."

"Just hope the food is good and inexpensive." Howard smiled as he grabbed his coat and went outside to start the car.

While Howard started the car, Ruth made a quick call to Marie. "Marie, pray to your Light. Howard is covered in ice and he doesn't believe me. I'm pretending not to see it. We are going to the P&R coffee shop for supper. I'm hoping the food is good and your waitress, Sally, is there. Maybe I can make a connection with her. Howard doesn't want me to come over to your house anymore."

Marie listened to her precious neighbor and encouraged her. "Ruth, I'll pray, get others to pray, and let Sally know you are coming."

"Thanks, Marie, I have to go."

"I understand. Bye."

Ruth put on a fake smile and got into the passenger seat of the Stantons's car. "I'm hungry, Howard. Thanks for taking me to dinner. It is a real treat for me."

"You really tricked me into this. I didn't know you had it in you," Howard replied, and then turned on the radio. Music filled the otherwise silent drive.

Right after Ruth's call, Marie texted Sally. *Are you working now?*

Sally texted back. *I got off at one today. What's happening?*

My neighbor, Ruth, started seeing ice and her husband thinks she is crazy and won't let her come to my home anymore. They are coming to the coffee shop for dinner. Could you somehow support her?

I can go back to the shop to help out. I'll tell Sam that he won't need to pay me. Judy, the waitress there now, wouldn't mind the help for a couple of hours. Sam will probably let Sarah and I have a free dinner for helping out, too. I'll go right now and ask Sarah to make some calls. Have a good visit with Rick this evening.

Thanks. You're a great friend.

Sally told Sarah what was going on as she put on her waitress uniform and went downstairs to help out in the coffee shop. Neither Sarah nor Sally had told Marie that they lived in one of the low-income apartments above the coffee shop. Theirs was a two-bedroom apartment which took up the whole fourth floor of the building. Sally was talking to Sam just as Ruth and Howard walked in. Judy was busy, so Sally walked over to the Stantons and invited them to sit at a booth near the displayed desserts.

Howard looked skeptical as he offered one side of the booth to his wife. "Why did you gasp when we parked the car? I do know how to parallel park, you know."

Ruth's thoughts whirled around as she thought how to answer. *There was ice on the outside of the building. This is scary. How am I going to keep this a secret?* She responded to her husband. "Howard, I just had a little heartburn. I am hungry."

Howard stared intently at Ruth, tightening the wrinkles on his labor-worn face, not saying anything. Ruth decided to go through with the meal and see if that changed anything.

Sally handed menus to Howard and Ruth along with ice water and a small plate of sliced lemons. "Can I get you anything else to drink as you look over the menu?"

"I suppose you don't have any beer," was Howard's response.

"You're right, sir, but we do have several choices of coffee, tea, sodas, flavored waters, and milks. A list is behind the napkin holder. Also, we have a special deal on our shaved prime rib melt or southwest chicken melt. You get any side for free if ordering it. I'll give you a couple of minutes to look over the menus."

Howard's tense face melted into a smile as he perused the menu. Ruth was glad that his mind for the moment was concentrating on food. "Wow, Ruth, if this stuff is as good as it sounds, we will be coming back. What do you want?"

Ruth had to prove she was hungry, so she replied, "I'm having the shaved prime rib melt and a side of home fries. And I want peach flavored water, too."

"Ruth, you never order so much. Are you having more of those menopause things going on?"

"Howard! We're out in public!"

Ruth was glad she could use menopause as a cover. Howard always became extra accommodating when she attributed mood changes to menopause.

"I'm sorry, dear. Let's enjoy this meal."

Howard motioned Sally over to order. "Miss, we'll have two of those shaved prime rib melts and two orders of home fries. And leave the bill open for desserts. I'll have the ginger ale and my wife wants the peach flavored water."

Sarah entered the coffee shop, hesitated, and went up to Ruth and Howard's table. "Is that you, Mrs. Stanton? I'm sorry to interrupt your time, but I had a friend who knows you from your Montessori teaching. She said that you were really a good teacher and wished that you still taught."

"Yes, dear, I am Mrs. Stanton, and I do miss teaching. Thank you for your compliment."

Sarah smiled and went up to Sally to ask if her dinner could be take-out.

Ruth had seen a glimpse of Sarah at Marie's house and now put things together in her mind. Montessori, Sarah, and Sally would be her connection to investigating the surreal ice.

Howard asked, "How can someone still be talking about your teaching when the Montessori school closed seven years ago?"

"My students remember me, Howard."

The meals were delivered with a joyful smile on Sally's face as she sincerely wished them, "Bon appetit."

Howard and Ruth each ordered a piece of New York cheesecake for dessert and did not take a doggie bag home. Howard was extremely pleased with the meal. Ruth was stuffed. She would sit on the couch next to her frozen husband at home as the meal settled. Perhaps Howard would not get sick like Rick.

Chapter 20

SUPPER AND REHAB CENTER

Marie made hamburgers for supper. They were easy and a favorite of Deb and Bobbie. Marie's mind swirled. *How am I going to continue? Please, Light, show me the way. Deb and I didn't have a chance to talk before supper.*

The phone signaled that a text came in. It was from Ruth.

Howard and I went to the P&R coffee shop and saw the waitress and her daughter. It was good. I will contact them to talk about the gray ice tomorrow. Howard seems fine even though that ice is all over him. The ice is everywhere in our home and it is getting cold. Howard doesn't understand it or see it. He started a fire in the fireplace. Where can I find this Light you talked about?

Marie texted back to Ruth. *Just start talking to the Light. He is everywhere and He will hear you. I will talk to Him, too. Do you think you need a doctor?*

No, but I'm afraid to go to sleep.

Text me if you need help.

Thank you.

After cleaning up, it was time to go to the rehab center. Marie turned to her daughter. "Deb, I want to take you and Bobbie with me tonight when we visit your dad. I'll watch Bobbie when you go to see your father and you can watch Bobbie when it's my turn."

"They probably won't let you in the waiting room with Bobbie."

"I go," Bobbie said, likely not even comprehending where they were going. He did enjoy riding in the car.

When they arrived at the hospital, personnel just thought that Bobbie was a patient. Marie knew where to go, and this helped with anyone who might question them. Rita was at the information desk and three other people were waiting to visit their loved ones.

"Hi, Rita. Is anyone visiting Rick now?"

"Dr. Willard is with Rick. What's your boy's name?

"Bobbie."

Rita bent down to Bobbie's level and stated, "Hi, Bobbie. You are so cute." Rita spoke to Marie, "He shouldn't be here, but I'm so glad you brought Bobbie. He gives me hope for my Alexandria."

"Alexandria is a beautiful name. My daughter, Deb, is twelve. Can she see her father?"

"You are supposed to be sixteen. Dr. Willard will be out soon. Perhaps he could go with Deb or watch Bobbie. Rick can see two people at a time now. He is improving."

The other people waiting were given permission to see their loved one. Rita escorted them.

Deb asked, "What was that all about, Mom? You should have left Bobbie and me at home."

"Rita has a preemie in the Neonatal ICU who might have cerebral palsy."

"That's not the same as Downs."

"Seeing a child with any disability will help her know that she is not alone."

Once Rita returned, Marie went up to the counter. "How is everything going with Alexandria?"

"I can't wait to hold her, to hear her voice, to just be her mom, but I'm afraid. I can't heal her or protect her and that makes me feel like a failure. I couldn't carry her to term. My boyfriend left. My mom is mad at me for getting pregnant. I just keep working and pumping milk and trying not to think. It's so hard. Sorry, I shouldn't lay this all on you. I really don't know you, except that you're a mom." Frozen tears formed again in Rita's eyes.

How does this poor young mom keep going?

Bobbie, who seemed to sense emotional needs in people, hugged Rita's legs.

Rita reached down and gently patted Bobbie's head.

Bobbie looked up at her and said, "Light, Light."

What does Bobbie understand? How can he know?

Rita looked at Marie quizzically. Marie responded to her silent question. "The Light is God's Son. His Name is Jesus. Several of us know Him as the Light. The Light has answered our prayers and done miracles in my life. I don't think Rick would be alive now if it wasn't for the Light."

Marie told her son, "Bobbie, you can go give Deb a hug now."

Bobbie looked up at Rita for permission.

"Go ahead, Bobbie, I'm okay. Go hug your sister."

Bobbie let go with another, "Light, Light."

Rita wiped her eyes and dealt with another visitor to the rehab center.

Dr. Willard came into the waiting room. "You are a courageous woman, Mrs. Winton, to bring your family despite the rules. But I break rules, too. Just don't tell anyone. I'll give Rita a break and take you all back to see Rick. He is awake, but speaking slowly."

Marie's somber, blank expression revealed her anxious heart as she picked up Bobbie and followed Dr. Willard, along with Deb, down the hall to Rick's room.

As soon as Marie put Bobbie down, he ran into the room and up to Rick's bed. The IVs didn't bother him. He crawled up onto the bed next to his dad.

Bobbie found Teddy covered up under the blanket and cried, "Teddy!"

Dr. Willard waited in the hall while Deb and Marie entered Rick's room.

Deb grabbed Marie's right elbow. Marie felt Deb's shaky hand and touched her daughter's hand with her own as they slowly walked together into the hospital room.

Rick's eyes were slightly open. He sensed Deb's presence and said softly, "De…b, I lo… ve y….ou."

Deb cried frozen tears, went to her dad, and kissed his forehead.

Marie joined her family, placing her right arm around Deb and holding Rick's hand with her left hand.

Bobbie said, "Light, Light."

Did Bobbie see light or did he just repeat the phrase? His words came at the right time.

Dr. Willard had been standing by the door. He gazed at Marie's family and prayed. The Light's presence filled the room. Marie quietly said the Lord's prayer. Somehow, the words came to her. She had memorized it as a child. "Our Father in heaven, hallowed be your name, your kingdom come, your will be done, on earth as it is in heaven. Give us today our daily bread.

And forgive us our debts, as we also have forgiven our debtors. And lead us not into temptation, but deliver us from the evil one."

Rick said "A … men."

Bobbie put Teddy back under the blanket for his dad. Rick said, "Tha….nk y…ou, Bo… bbie."

They stayed a few more minutes. Marie put her finger on Rick's lips to quiet him. It took a lot of effort for him to speak. Finally, they each kissed Rick on his forehead.

Deb and Bobbie said, "Bye, Daddy; love you."

Dr. Willard met them at the door and said, "There is a diner across the street. Could I buy you all a dessert and we'll have a talk about Rick?"

Bobbie corrected the doctor and said, "Daddy."

Chapter 21

KELSEY'S DINER

Kelsey's diner was an old railroad car transformed into a small restaurant. The inside had white walls with pictures of trains near the ceiling. The kitchen was along one long side. Royal blue booths with white laminate tables lined the opposite side. A few stools stood along the counter next to the kitchen with royal blue seat cushions. Two people were working the evening shift.

As Bobbie entered the dinner, he exclaimed, "Cookies!" A display of a variety of large specialty cookies sat on the counter next to the register opposite the entry door.

Dr. Willard asked, "How about hot chocolate with a cookie?"

Bobbie's eyes opened wide in surprise as he squeaked, "For me."

Dr. Willard guided the family to one of the booths.

He asked Deb, "What can I get for you, Deb? They have other desserts. I love the raspberry turnovers."

"I don't want anything." Deb sat like a frozen statue. The muscles on her face constricted into a stiff scowl.

"Marie, what would you like?"

"Could they make toast at this time in the evening?"

"Let's ask. Excuse me, Mia, besides desserts, can you make toast at this time in the evening?"

"Dr. Willard, you are such a good customer, I will personally make toast. Which would you like, whole wheat or Italian bread?"

"Italian or whole wheat, Marie, and how many?"

"I'd like three pieces of Italian bread toasted with hot chocolate."

Dr. Willard said, "Okay, Mia, here is my order: three pieces of Italian bread toasted with butter and any jam you have, two raspberry turnovers, three hot chocolates, one coffee with cream and sugar, and one of each of the cookies on display."

Bobbie piped up, "For me!"

Dr. Willard faced Bobbie at Bobbie's level. "You can pick one cookie for now, and the rest your mom will take home for later this week." Dr. Willard insisted on paying no matter how much Marie protested.

Their booth was the farthest from the door so conversation could be private. Mia put the cookies in a container for the Wintons to take home minus the one Bobbie chose. Since he liked red and chocolate, Bobbie chose the red velvet cookie with chocolate chunks. Marie was sure that the cookie and the hot chocolate would keep Bobbie awake for a while.

After receiving their food, Dr. Willard began, "Marie, Rick is recovering nicely. Even though he had a TIA, I don't believe he will be impacted physically like his dad. He just began communicating today. We won't know about anything else until he gets further along in his recovery over the next few weeks."

Deb spoke up, "If my dad doesn't get all the way well, I'm not going to trust the Light for anything."

Bobbie said, "Light, Light."

Deb grumbled, 'Shut up!"

Bobbie cried and stopped eating.

Dr. Willard seemed to understand both of Marie's children. He directed his attention to Bobbie. "Bobbie, it seems like your sister could use a hug. She has done a lot for you."

Bobbie took the remainder of his cookie, gave it to Deb, and put his arms around his sister as best as he could.

Deb could not resist his hug. The cookie crumbled. Dr. Willard bought another red velvet cookie, divided it in half, and gave half to Deb and half to Bobbie. Marie's children sat hugging each other and eating their cookie. Deb even drank the extra hot chocolate which had been ordered for her.

Dr. Willard told the Wintons why he had taken them to Kelsey's diner. "As you know, I am not Rick's doctor in the rehab center. Dr. Stevens is a good doctor. Rick is under his care. Since he doesn't do rounds during the evening visiting time, it is hard to reach him with any questions you may have. Dr. Stevens's office will inform my office of Rick's progress. You can call my office and get updates during my business hours which are 8:30 to 5:00 Monday through Friday. If an emergency comes up, the rehab center will contact my office and you directly. I have informed my office staff that you, Marie, and Rick's parents can be given updates. If you would like me to visit Rick as a friend or work with him after he is released, you can call my office with your request. I have enjoyed meeting and working with all of you. I just have many patients and a wife who wants to see me once in a while."

Deb asked, "Why can't I get updates?"

"The updates have to go to an adult, Deb. I'm sure that your mom will let you know what they are. You can also call your grandparents. Jane visited Rick this afternoon. Her name was on the visitors' log."

Marie touched Dr. Willard's hand. "You have done so much for us. You got Rick the help he needed in time and taught me more about the Light. You will always be special to our family. If Rick needs help following after he gets out of rehab, I will certainly call you. Could we pray for Rick now and for Ruth?"

"Who is Ruth?"

"She is my neighbor and sees the gray ice now, but her husband doesn't see it."

Deb then said, "Maybe this is a virus like Mr. Miller said and has nothing to do with you know who."

Deb's words struck Marie's heart like an arrow.

Dr. Willard asked Deb, "How did you find me, Deb?"

"Sarah and Sally knew you."

"How did you find Sarah and Sally?"

"My mom wanted to go into the P&R coffee shop because she said that she prayed to the Light."

"Why was your mom praying to the Light?"

Deb sighed. "Because Grandma Jane told us to look for the Light, and Roger told her to talk to the Light."

"Why did Sarah and Sally tell you about me?"

Deb began to put these thoughts together. "Because Sarah knew me and Sally knew my dad."

"If you hadn't gone with your mom to look for the Light, your dad might not be recovering right now. Deb, the Light used you to help your dad. The Light, that is Jesus, loves you both."

Bobbie listened and said, "Light, Light, Jesus, Jesus."

Dr. Willard smiled. "Let's pray. Bobbie, you can pray, too."

They all held hands as Dr. Willard prayed. "Father, You are so good to us. You brought the Light into our lives. We ask tonight that You would bring healing to Rick and Ruth and guidance to this family so that they may all find rest in your presence. In the Name of the Light. Amen.

Bobbie said, "Light, Light, Amen, Amen."

Dr. Willard drained his coffee cup. "Marie, I feel that Ruth will find her way, but give her my number and let me know if she needs my assistance."

They thanked Mia for the food. Dr. Willard paid the bill, and they all headed home.

Chapter 22

RUTH AND DEB

As soon as Marie got home, she got Bobbie ready for bed. The effect of the sugar was wearing off. "Deb, I'm going to sit up for a while. Would you like to stay up with me?"

"That depends on what you're going to do."

"We could talk for a while." *I need to talk to Deb about my meetings with Megan, and Jacobs's Grocery.*

"I'm tired of talking. I think I'll go to bed and read."

"Ok. I love you."

"Love you, too." Deb retreated into her cold room.

Marie searched through the books on the bookshelf. There were a lot of books on home maintenance, health remedies, and mystery novels. She found the old book about the Light and opened it.

Where do I begin? There must be something in here that will help me be a better parent for Deb and Bobbie. I also have to call Sally.

Marie's cell phone signaled a text message had come. She took the phone out of her pocket to see who it was. *Marie, this is Ruth. I saw your car turn into your driveway. Are the children in bed?*

Yes, Marie texted back.

Could you sit up with me and text back and forth for a while? I need to get rid of this ice and cold.

I can sit up with you. You can't get rid of the murky gray ice yourself. You need the Light.

I listened to your story, but don't understand who or what the Light is.

Marie remembered Jane talking about the book of John, so, she looked up John in the book about the Light called the Bible and texted Ruth. Do you have a Bible?

No.

I will loan you mine. I will go out and put it in your mailbox. Will you be able to go out and get it?

Yes. I'll give anything a try.

Ok. Start with the book of John. I'll pray for you. Marie wrapped the Bible up in a grocery bag and went outside to put it in Ruth's mailbox.

Deb must have heard Marie leave. She was standing in the kitchen when Marie came back into the house. "Mom, where did you go?!"

"I loaned Ruth the book about the Light."

"Mom, you are really scaring me. You are turning into a Light Freak and I'm going to lose you." Marie wrapped Deb in her arms. "You are not going to lose me or your dad or Bobbie. We are a family. I do believe in the Light because I have seen Him and felt His love. That doesn't change my love for you."

"Why doesn't Bobbie see the ice?"

"I don't see the ice anymore either. The Light took it away when I asked Him to forgive me for the things I did that were not right."

Deb pulled away. "What? You don't see any ice. So, this is some kind of a curse on me and Ruth and other rejected people."

"You are not rejected. You are loved."

"I know, and special to whom?"

"The Light, God, me, Bobbie, your dad …"

Deb held her head in her hands. "I don't want to be a freak, but I'll give God or the Light a challenge. If Dad can make a full sentence without any hesitating tomorrow, I'll ask the Light to show me what I need forgiveness for." Deb went to her room.

Marie prayed over and over again. *Please Creator, please Light, help Deb to know how much You love her and for Rick to make a full sentence. Help Ruth to understand what she is reading and be healed of the ice.* It was getting late, but Marie had to call Sally.

"Hello."

"Sally, this is Marie. I'm sorry to call so late."

"I'm not in bed yet, and your phone calls are always welcome. It went very well today with Ruth and Howard at the coffee shop. When Sarah made calls to friends to pray, one of her friends remembered Mrs. Staton from the Montessori School. Sarah came into the coffee shop and went up to Ruth to give her a compliment on her teaching. Ruth had seen Sarah at your home when she brought blankets over. Ruth knows the connection with us. Isn't the Light cool!"

"That's wonderful. But I have a question. Do you have any ideas about how to handle the situation at the middle school?"

"I was able to check out material the Baptist school uses and compare it to Sarah's work from school, along with conversations with her. The main emphasis in the public school material is on gaining knowledge through the lens of current cultural norms. The Christian material has a foundation of Biblical truth which applies to every subject."

Marie bit her lip. "School isn't the only problem. Deb said that she won't believe in the Light unless Rick says a sentence without hesitating." Tears rolled down Marie's face as she haltingly got out her words of concern. "Could you … pray for Deb?"

"Of course. Dear Father, Deb is on our hearts tonight. You know what is best for her. Help us to trust you and calm Marie's anxiety. In the Name of the Light. Amen."

"Marie, the Light has carried my family through many tough times. I know He will continue to carry our family whether I understand the situation or not. He will do the same for you. Because of Him, you are the Creator's child under His care. I believe the Light is working on a major miracle for both of us and our families. I believe Ruth will be part of it. You need to get some rest."

Exhausted, Marie went to bed. *I will tell Deb about the psychologist appointment in the morning.*

Help me to trust You, Light. I'm so used to controlling things myself.

Chapter 23

NEW BEGINNINGS

A cardinal's singing woke Marie at 8AM. She had slept through the night without dreaming. Perhaps this would be a good day. She reached over to Rick's side of the bed still expecting him to be there. Sadness was softened by the knowledge that he was recovering. Morning light shone through the windows drawing Marie out of bed and beckoning her to view the sun-splashed sight outside. Only a few areas of snow remained with green grass poking through the snow crystals. Purple edged the sidewalk. *Crocuses! Flowers without frosted edges!* Marie's heart joined the voice of the cardinal.

Bobbie must be awake now. Marie threw on a robe and descended the stairs ending in the kitchen. *When was last time I actually looked at our back yard?* A few steps brought Marie to the window. French lilacs bordered the left edge of the yard. They were not yet in bloom, but seemed to have a light purple hue on the branches promising new life. The right and back border were defined by neighbors' white fences. A swing set sat in the corner by the fences. *Wait! Someone was on the swing. Bobbie!*

It didn't matter if Marie was dressed for the day or not. *Bobbie has never ventured outside by himself before.* She rushed outside calling, "Bobbie!"

Bobbie came running toward his mom saying, "I did it! I did it!"

Marie had no idea that two of Bobbie's goals were to get outside by himself and get on the swing by himself. Bobbie held his mom's hand as he guided her to the swing and demonstrated his accomplishment.

"You are a good swinger, Bobbie."

"Swinger, Swinger."

"Bobbie, when you want to go outside, you have to tell Deb or me. I know you are a big boy and can open the door, but I want to know where you are."

Bobbie looked at Marie with those searching blue eyes. "Bobbie big."

"Well, big boy, let's go wake up Deb." *How was I to prevent Bobbie from letting himself outside?* Bobbie ran ahead in order to get to Deb's room first. *Will he be able to open the door to get inside?* Bobbie used both hands to twist the knob. He had learned a new skill all by himself.

The door to Deb's room was off the kitchen just before entering the living room. Bobbie rushed up to it, but it didn't push open. Deb had a latch on the inside of her door which she must have hooked when she went to bed last night.

Marie gently called, "Deb."

Bobbie wasn't as gentle. "Debbie … Debbie … Debbie."

"I'm tired. Go away."

Bobbie kept knocking. Marie told Bobbie to stop. "I have some things we need to talk about this morning, Deb. I'll let you sleep for another hour and then we can have breakfast and talk."

Bobbie pouted. "I sad."

"Bobbie, would you like to make breakfast with me?" Since food was especially important to Bobbie, his sad countenance changed to one of joy. Together, they got out a muffin mix that Jane had purchased for them. Bobbie added the oil while Marie added the egg. They both mixed the batter.

While the batter baked, Marie put a children's story tape in the VCR called "The Cat in the Hat" by Dr. Suess. The story was almost over when Deb came out of her room.

"Mom, did you have to play that this morning?"

Bobbie sang, "Cat, hat, cat, hat."

Deb looked like she was in the mood for a fight, but too tired to have one.

"What do you have to talk to me about, Mom?"

"Let's eat breakfast first and get dressed. Then we can talk while Bobbie is occupied with his handheld game."

Deb retreated to her room to get dressed.

Bobbie never missed anything. "Game, game."

"Not now, Bobbie. After breakfast." Marie didn't dare go upstairs to get dressed until Deb came out of her room as Bobbie might decide to go outside again. A few minutes later, Deb joined Bobbie in the living room. Marie asked, "Deb, could you take the muffins out of the oven when the timer rings? I need to get dressed. Stay with Bobbie until I come down. He can open the outside door by himself now."

Deb sat with her brother while Marie went upstairs. Their whole world was changing. *Light, next week I'll start working. I'm scared. I don't want to leave Deb and Bobbie.*

The muffins had just come out of the oven when Marie got downstairs. *Thank you, Light, for sending a repair man for the stove while I was at the rehab center. Jane and Lee have connections I did not know about.*

They ate in silence. Bobbie took his muffins into the living room to finish another Dr. Suess story.

"Deb, when I picked up the subject material for you at the middle school, Mr. Miller called me into his office. Mr. Miller and Mrs. Harris want you to see the school psychologist."

"Well, that's not going to happen."

"No, it's not. I talked to Megan at the Becker School. She said that the middle school can demand that you see a psychologist, but it doesn't have to be the school psychologist. Megan set up an appointment for today with a nice man who is a psychologist, but we can go together. That way we can fulfill the demand of the school without putting you into their hands."

"But I still have to see a psychologist?"

"Yes, but only to fulfill the reported concern from the middle school. Otherwise, a state agency could start to investigate our family."

"Why did you take me there in the first place?"

"It's what the social worker at the rehab center said I had to do. Deb, I am looking into other educational possibilities. Ruth Stanton used to teach at the Montessori school. She was going to check into state laws for homeschooling. She and some other retired teachers may be able to organize a homeschool program for you. The Christian school costs too much."

"Mrs. Stanton is okay as long as it is here and not in her house. But what about her husband? He's mean and doesn't like kids. And how long will it take for Mrs. Stanton to be ready to teach?"

"I don't know. But many things are falling into place. I believe that the Light will guide us. We can look at the material the middle school teachers gathered for you and see what they are teaching at least. I do have a job with the Becker School, and Bobbie can go to preschool there. I also have a job on Saturdays at Jacobs's Grocery Store. Grandpa Lee said that you and Bobbie can go to their house on Saturdays. Your Uncle Ken and Aunt Sophia are moving back here in a month and they may be able to help out some, too, at least for Saturdays. I don't start work until next week."

"It looks like you got everyone taken care of, except me."

"Deb, I am working on it. I don't want you to go to the middle school, either, but if that is the only option, then we have to keep on top of everything so they can't come against our family. I am hopeful that Ruth will be able to work something out. I want us to go to church on Sunday with your Nana Jane. People there might have some ideas for schooling as well."

"I'm going to watch the movie with Bobbie."

"Deb, I love you."

There was no response from Deb.

Marie picked up the phone and called Sally's number. *I hadn't asked her to pray about the school form or the psychologist appointment for Deb.*

"Hello, who am I talking to?"

"Sally, it's me, Marie."

"Marie, how are you? I've been thinking about you and all the stuff you have to go through."

"Sally, I'm really concerned about Deb going to the middle school. There is a form that Mr. Miller gave me giving permission for the school psychologist to evaluate Deb. They think the surreal ice we've seen are hallucinations. Based on that, they believe that they have the right to investigate our family."

"I don't like Sarah going there either, but the Christian school is so expensive. It seems like being anti-Christian is a criterion for employment at the public school. The new school psychologist is pushing to get all students who follow the Light to be evaluated. Parents are being asked to sign a consent form."

"Did you sign the consent form?"

"No. Other parents are calling me from the teen group. None of us have signed."

"I am taking Deb to a private psychologist who is evaluating Deb today. Megan from the Becker School set it up. He is a believer."

"That's great. What is his name? When are you seeing him?"

"Dr. Michael Hill. This afternoon at 3:00."

"That's wonderful news. Why don't you and Deb and Bobbie come to the coffee shop for an early supper? I've told Sam about you, I'm sure we could arrange a free meal. I'm anxious to hear how everything goes if you or Deb want to talk. Besides, you need to eat before going to see Rick."

"I'll let you know. It will depend on how Deb feels."

"Marie, I'm not sending Sarah to school today because of the push for a psychological evaluation. Could you mention that Deb is not the only teen from Christian families whom the school wants to evaluate?"

"I could, but Dr. Hill couldn't possibly see them all."

"There are about 13 teens who only come to the teen group, not to church. There are 32 teens who go to churches in town. We are planning a meeting with all these teens, their parents, and their pastors on Saturday at 10AM in the Baptist Christian School cafeteria. Maybe Dr. Hill could come and give us some guidance."

"I've never met him. I'll invite him if it feels right."

"That's a good idea. Listen to the Light. Not all the teens are believers in the Light, but none of them want to see the school psychologist."

"I'll be there on Saturday. It is my last free Saturday, and I need a support group."

Just as Sally and Marie said their good-byes, Jane called.

"Marie, Lee said that you called. Saturdays are fine. There is a new playground at the Catholic school down the street. Bobbie will love that."

"Thanks, Jane, for all your help. How are your legs?"

"They're old, but they still work. I just won't ever be a rocket."

"Jane, I won't ever be a rocket either. Now tell me the truth. Is everything okay?"

"I just have arthritis and poor circulation. The doctor wants me to eat better, get more sleep, and more exercise like the rest of humanity."

"Now I don't feel bad about sending Deb and Bobbie to your house on Saturdays. You will definitely get exercise with them. Jane, could you possibly watch Bobbie tomorrow? There is a meeting about this form parents have to sign requiring students to see the psychologist if they say anything about the surreal ice. I want to go to the meeting with Deb."

"When and where is the meeting?"

"10 o'clock at the Baptist School cafeteria. Why do you ask?"

"I have connections. Every church with a prayer line and the local Christian radio station will have this information within the hour. Somewhere in the Bible it says that a three-fold cord is not easily broken. Let's see if the Light will multiply that by 100."

"Jane, you are amazing. I think I'll call Ruth and tell her. If I tell Ruth and Dr. Hill, maybe they will invite others."

"Who is Dr. Hill? Is anyone sick?" Marie assured Jane that everyone was well and explained about the upcoming visit to Dr. Hill's office. Then she texted Ruth, not wanting to cause any problem with Howard if he was home.

Ruth there is a meeting about a required form parents have to sign giving the middle school the right to demand students who have hallucinations to see the school psychologist. Parents and some community residents are concerned and are having a meeting at the Baptist School cafeteria tomorrow at 10 o'clock. – Just letting you know if you want to go.

Ruth texted back. *I'll be there.* Marie had no idea what Ruth was going through.

Chapter 24

DR. HILL

After a lunch of bologna sandwiches and sliced apples, the Wintons all got ready to go to Dr. Hill's office. Marie made a quick call to the rehab center to check on Rick.

"Rehab center. Can I help you?"

"This is Marie Winton. I'm calling to see if there are any updates on Rick Winton."

"I'll check." Classical music played on the line for a moment. "Mrs. Winton, Dr. Stevens ordered an MRI today and some bloodwork. Mr. Winton is a little more responsive today, so, you may visit for up to 20 minutes during visiting hours."

"Thank you." Hope again was rising in Marie's heart. *Thank you, Light.*

At 2:00 PM the Wintons got in the car and drove to McKinney Drive. Bobbie relished every moment of the trip. Every stoplight was, "Light, Light." He imitated every dog's bark or loud noise for their enjoyment.

Dr. Hill's office was in an older home with a stone façade and a large building-wide porch. Marie parked behind the building and entered the building through the front door, which was in the middle of the veranda. Just inside the foyer to the right was a large waiting room with a fireplace, a couch, and four chairs separated by end tables. It felt more like someone's living room than the waiting room for a doctor's office. To the left, another large room contained two desks, files and a cheerful secretary. An English cocker spaniel stood wagging her tail greeting the Wintons with a barking type of hello.

Bobbie couldn't contain himself, saying "Sandy, Sandy" as he ran to pet the dog.

"That's not Sandy," corrected Deb.

Bobbie paid no attention to his sister as he petted the cocker's nose.

"Hello, I'm Olivia," the secretary said. "Max loves kids. She is also a trained therapy dog. There's nothing to worry about. You must be the Wintons. Dr. Hill will be with you in just a couple of minutes. Why don't you relax in the waiting room? Your son is welcome to stay here and pet Max."

"Thank you. I'm Marie. This is Deb and Bobbie."

"It's nice to meet you." Marie returned the same gesture and started to the waiting room, when Dr. Hill came out of his office. He stopped to pet Max and say hello to Bobbie before speaking to Deb and Marie.

"Mrs. Winton and Deb, it is a pleasure to meet you. Meagan from the Becker School has given me a little background about your situation. Bobbie can stay with Max and Olivia while I speak with both of you."

Marie knelt down next to Bobbie. "Bobbie, Deb and I are going to talk to Dr. Hill. You need to take care of Max while we talk."

Bobbie looked at his mom quizzically. "Bobbie go, too."

Dr. Hill came to their rescue. "Okay. Max and Bobbie can come in while we talk as a family."

Dr. Hill's office had three very comfortable overstuffed chairs arranged in a semicircle in the front of his large cherry desk. Bookcases ran along one wall filled with not only books for all ages, but with stuffed animals and games. There were also boxes of toys for children and dogs. Max ran to the box of dog toys.

Bobbie stood entranced. Suddenly he screeched, "Teddy!" Sitting on the bookcase between Winnie the Pooh and Cat in the Hat books sat a teddy bear just like Bobbie's bear. Bobbie ran to the shelf and hugged the teddy bear. He then said, "Daddy."

Deb was the first to respond to Bobbie's outburst. "Bobbie, Teddy has a twin. There are two teddys. Daddy has one and Dr. Hill has one."

Bobbie put the teddy bear back and sat down quietly by the bookcase. Max trotted over to Bobbie, sat down, and licked Bobbie's face. Bobbie put his left hand on the back of Max's neck and Max put his paw on Bobbie's lap.

Everyone seemed surprised at Bobbie's sad continence. Dr. Hill went over and sat on the floor next to Bobbie. He was silent for a few moments. He then took the teddy from the shelf and hugged it. "Teddy makes me feel better."

Bobbie said, "Teddy is Daddy's."

"Could your daddy use two teddies?"

Bobbie's eyes got huge. "Two!'

"Yes, two. I would really like to give your daddy my teddy. Could you give it to your daddy for me?"

Bobbie climbed up onto Dr. Hill's lap and hugged him. Max licked them both. After a couple of minutes, Dr. Hill asked Bobbie, "Can I talk to Deb and your mom now?"

Bobbie got off Dr. Hill's lap with teddy firmly under his left arm and held his hand out to Dr. Hill. Dr. Hill took Bobbie's hand as Bobbie led him over to Deb and Marie. Then Bobbie went over to the toy box to investigate what was there while never dropping this new teddy.

Dr. Hill began, "I would like to talk with both of you, but before that, I want you to take ten minutes to write down what has happened in the last week and how you feel about it. I'll read what you wrote and then talk to both of you. Do this independent of each other. During that time, I'm going to open the door to the office and ask Olivia to play with Max and Bobbie in the office."

Bobbie's ears caught the mention of his name.

Dr. Hill sent a message to Olivia and handed both Marie and Deb a notebook to write in. Olivia opened the door and spoke to Bobbie.

"Oh, Bobbie, you look like you could use a cookie. Max needs a cookie, too."

At the sound of the word, "cookie," Max ran into the office. Bobbie laughed and followed Max. Olivia gave them both their respective treats while she dragged the box of toys into the office. She left the door just a little ajar.

After the writing was completed, Dr. Hill read both reports. He then addressed both Deb and Marie. "I want you to know that you are not the only family contacting me with this issue at the middle school. I am also familiar with the report form requesting a psychological evaluation. By coming here, you are replacing the school psychologist with a private psychologist, but the school psychologist can still submit concerns to me. Everything you share with me is confidential. I will need your written permission to share any of it with insurance and the school psychologist. Do you have any questions before we start?"

Deb spoke, "Why do they feel I need an evaluation?"

"Good question. "Deb, you have experienced a lot of changes in your life in just a week's time without the space to adjust to them. Pressure from the school to enroll and adjust to their expectations would naturally cause some oppositional behavior. You are a very smart, insightful young lady, and I can tell that you love your family very much. May I ask you a question?"

"Sure."

"Can you tell me what things you feel you are losing control of?"

Deb put on a defensive posture. "It's obvious. I can't make my dad well. I can't be taught at home. People are taking over my space and forcing me to go to that dumb middle school. No one cares about me. I can take care of myself and Bobbie."

"Does the gray ice bother you?"

"Mom doesn't see it any more. Bobbie never saw it. I see it because it is my fault it came."

"That is a lot to deal with for anyone. Deb, I'm going to ask your mom the same question. Marie, what things do you feel you are losing control of?"

"I can't heal my husband. I can't be home and work at the same time. I can't figure out how to provide schooling for Deb.

I don't want her to go to the middle school. The ice isn't Deb's fault, it's mine. And, I can't convince Deb to trust the Light."

Deb jumped up and said, "Light, Light, Light—I'm tired of hearing it!"

From the office came Bobbie's voice, "Light, Light."

Deb groaned.

Dr. Hill was silent for a couple of minutes allowing Deb and Marie to regain emotional composure and then addressed them. "Each of you have had a traumatic experience. It is evident that you love each other and are facing considerable changes in your lives. First of all, we need to let go of the things we can't control. Neither of you can heal Mr. Winton. Neither one of you are responsible for his condition. You may have said things or thought things or even done things that made Mr. Winton sad or affected his behavior, but those things did not cause his illness. The ice is not controlled by either of you."

Deb sat with frozen tears on her cheeks.

Dr. Hill continued, "However, what you say and do in Mr. Winton's presence now could help him in his recovery."

Deb looked at Dr. Hill and asked, "Like what?"

"Show him that you and your mom and Bobbie are a team working together for the good of his family."

"How do we do that?"

"We have to first give up the things we can't control.

"Marie, I can sense your concern for Deb. Deb is a very responsible, bright twelve-year-old and she needs space to figure out some things in her own time. Deb, your mom has had a very special spiritual experience with the 'L-i-g-h-t'. She wants you to have the same experience because it has brought peace and hope to her. Do you both understand this?"

Deb and Marie nodded. "Can you think of ways to respect each other in regards to this issue?"

Marie reached out and touched Deb's hand. "I'm sorry for putting pressure on you. I love you so much that I want you to know the 'L-i-g-h-t', but it is your decision to make, not mine for you. I can't stop being who I am. I will give you space to be who you are. Will you help me?"

Deb gave Marie a hug. "I'm sorry, Mom. I just get so frustrated with everything and I feel cornered, especially after having Sarah and her mom over."

Dr. Hill asked, "Who is Sarah?"

Deb let her bitterness show. "She used to be a friend and then was really mean to Bobbie. That's when I left school. All of a sudden, she shows up when we looked for the 'L-i-g-h-t' wanting me to forgive her. Then she comes to my house and takes over playing with Bobbie. She has no right."

"So, you've never let go of your hate for her."

"Why should I?"

"Does hating her make you feel better?"

"Yes. No. I don't know."

"Marie, Deb needs some space to deal with her feelings. I suggest that you wait until Deb invites Sarah over to your home. However, Deb, if you see Sarah in school or other places, you must treat her without judgment. Do you both agree with this?"

They each hesitantly agreed. *I would have to tell Sally.*

"Let's return to the 'L-i-g-h-t' issue. You've made progress today by sharing your feelings. There will still be hurdles. I suggest that attending a good church would help both of you. That way, the message you, Marie, want Deb to hear is from a preacher, and Deb, the message is less than an hour once a week. Besides that, you don't have to live with the preacher." Smiling acceptance reflected in both their faces.

"Now, let's attack this school situation. Remember, this is a team effort. Deb, your mom is required by law to send you to school or provide an accepted alternative. When your mom homeschooled you, she used material that she had to present to the school district for their approval. She now has to work to provide financially for your family. I know your mom has investigated every possible way she can think of to prevent you from going to the public school. There may be other possibilities. Unfortunately, these take time."

"Mrs. Stanton, our neighbor, may be able to homeschool me."

"She will have to file papers with the state and the school district along with the materials she plans to use. She has to be a certified teacher since she is not a relative."

Marie spoke up. "Dr. Hill, Ruth was a Montessori school teacher with a desire to teach. She could be a person to help with Deb's education, however, she has just started seeing the surreal ice. ...Oh, and Sally McCain asked me to let you know that there will be a meeting this Saturday at 10 o'clock at the Baptist school for Christian parents who are concerned about the form we have to sign."

Dr. Hill let out a sigh. "I have seen the form the school psychologist wants parents to sign. It has a clause relating to the surreal ice which some people see and states, 'If the student refers to any hallucinations while on school grounds, such student will be referred for psychological evaluation and the family of such student will be interviewed as to the cause of these hallucinations.' Meagan told me about the form. According to our state, any school requiring psychological treatment for a child, may use a private psychologist of the family's choice rather than the school psychologist. So, you are encouraged to write my name on the form as your psychologist before signing it. I plan on starting a group therapy session for parents who add my name. I will have to charge a fee for this in order for it to be accepted as authentic."

"How much is the fee?"

"Twenty dollars per group session."

"We will do it. Are you planning on coming to the meeting?"

"I can go, but I can't take any more than 15 students. That would be three groups."

Deb had been quietly listening. "So, do I have to go to the middle school?"

"You will have to go until your mom figures out something else. This is part of working as a team. There are other people trying to figure out an answer to this as well. Your mom and you can connect with some of them on Saturday. Deb, remember, there are some things we can't control and some things we can. You can be brave and even be an example to other students. Your mom needs your help in this."

"But I don't want to go. I would rather run away!"

Marie sobbed uncontrollably, preventing her from saying anything.

Deb's steely expression melted into a heartbroken concern for her mom. Frozen tears slid down Deb's checks.

Dr. Hill spoke to Deb. "Your mom, your dad, and Bobbie need you. It is a lot of responsibility for you to carry. Where would you go if you ran away? You are a very important part of the Winton family team."

Deb rose from her chair and hugged her mom. "Mom, I'm so sorry. I didn't mean it. I won't leave you and Bobbie."

"I won't leave you either." The office had gotten quiet.

Dr. Hill sensed the need. He stood and opened the office door.

Bobbie was crying. Bobbie ran into Dr. Hill's office and put his little hands out to hold both Deb's and Marie's hands. Bobbie crawled up on his mom's lap trying not to let go of Deb's hand.

Deb moved to help him out.

Dr. Hill said, "See? You are a team."

Deb then bravely confessed, "I will go to the middle school and help Mom look for a better place for me to go. Maybe it won't have to be for long. I won't like it, but I will try."

Bobbie said, "Me, too."

"I have really enjoyed meeting with you. How about one more free appointment after your first week of school, next Friday at 4:30? I'll let Olivia know."

Deb and Marie thanked Dr. Hill, and Bobbie gave him a hug making sure not to drop the second teddy.

Chapter 25

RUTH'S BOLD DECISION

Ruth retrieved the Bible Marie had left for her in her mailbox. She spent the entire night reading through the gospels of Matthew, Mark, Luke, and John looking up all the cross references. *The Light Marie talks about must be Jesus. I've read the Lord's prayer. Maybe I'll try that.* Ruth began, "Our Father in heaven." Ruth stopped. *Could God be my father? I believe that God created this world, but my father? Maybe that means that God created me. But father means so much more than creator. It means someone who takes care of his child and protects his child."*

"God, if you are truly my father, please show me." Ruth turned to the first chapter of John. In the 12th verse it said, "Yet to all who did receive him, to those who believed in His Name, He gave the right to become children of God."

Ruth started again: "Our Father in heaven, hallowed be Your Name. Your Kingdom come, Your will be done on earth as it is in heaven."

It makes sense that You are holy. I don't know what Your Kingdom means, but heaven must be a lot better than earth.

"Forgive us our debts as we also have forgiven our debtors." Ruth's heart broke here. "Father, Jesus, I've been deceitful to Howard. I've been harboring bitterness about not teaching anymore because the Montessori school closed. I feel so guilty about turning Marie away when she needed the phone."

Then Ruth saw it. A Blue Light ray came through her kitchen window near where she was sitting. Ruth got up and looked into the living room. The ice was gone. She felt warmed and whispered, "I believe. Thank You Light, Jesus, Father, the only true God for forgiving me and taking away the ice. Help Howard to believe, too."

Howard woke expecting to see Ruth staying in bed while he got dressed for work. He would likely think that she was fixing his breakfast. Howard found Ruth in the kitchen dressed in the same clothes she had worn the previous day.

"What's wrong, Ruth?" Howard was genuinely concerned.

"Howard, I was reading the Bible and I prayed. I love you, Howard, and I haven't treated you right. Sometimes, I'm not honest with you. I did see the ice. It is gone now because Jesus took it away. Jesus is the Light. He is real. He forgave me for all the things that I've messed up. I was bitter about the Montessori school closing, too, and having to just stay home. Please forgive me, Howard."

Howard didn't know what to do. "Ruth, you could always apply for a job in the public school. I don't mind your working. Maybe that would be good for you. I don't know about this Jesus thing, but I'm glad you don't see ice. I've got to get to work. Please be normal when I get home—and get some sleep." Poor Howard probably wondered if menopause was making Ruth crazy.

An impossible idea started to fill Ruth with anticipation. She got on the phone and called the city hall as soon as it was open. *Maybe the Montessori school building could be opened again.* The city clerk answered the phone and transferred Ruth to the buildings and grounds department who then transferred her to the real estate department. The Montessori building had been empty for seven years. The city had tried to rent it out several times, but no one was interested. The building also had been listed for sale for over a year with no takers. The city simply wanted to get the building off their list of properties that had to be kept up according to city requirements. Ruth asked, "How much does it cost the city to keep the property up? If someone else did the upkeep, how much rent would be charged? What is the list price for the building currently?"

The clerk Ruth talked to gave her the answers that she was able to locate. "Upkeep is about $8,000 a year for that property. The last rent the city asked for was $1,600 per month. The building is currently listed at $175,000. Are you interested in this property? An agent who works with Beckerville City Property can set up a time to show you the building."

Ruth responded, "I would like to set up a time next week." The clerk agreed to get back to Ruth with a time to show her the building.

Maybe there is a way I can teach again in that same building. Ruth called a couple of the former Montessori school teachers and, with unbridled courage, called Pastor Richard Barnet of Faith Baptist Church.

Chapter 26

OUR TEAM

After the Wintons left Dr. Hill's office, Marie called Sally and thanked her for the meal offer, but told her that it would be better to take her up on the offer at a different time.

"Mom, why did you give up that free dinner?"

"We need to have time alone with each other before going to see your dad. Having a little space is good for today."

Deb gave her mom a hug and Bobbie joined in.

"So, what are we going to eat?"

"Let's stop by Jacobs's Grocery and get a sub and chips. Then, we can go home and eat our supper together before going to see your dad."

The groceries had to be charged, but Marie did get her 10% off thanks to Ron and Jack and Mr. Jacobs. Deb and Bobbie set the table. It felt good for just the three of them to eat supper together. Deb didn't even mind Marie saying grace.

At 6:30 PM, they headed for the hospital. Bobbie again said, "Light, light," at every stoplight and held tightly onto the new teddy he wanted to give to his dad.

Rita was at the reception desk when the Wintons entered. She looked worn out.

"Hi, Rita. Are you okay?"

Rita smiled. "It's good to see all of you." Frozen tears were in Rita's eyes.

Deb saw the tears and realized that Rita had the same problem she had. Deb was very quiet as Marie spoke to Rita.

"What's wrong, Rita? How is Alexandria?"

"Alexandria is doing well and gaining weight. She should be out of the neonatal ICU in about six weeks. My mom refuses to watch her when I work. I don't have anyone else. I have to prove that I can provide care for her when I am working. The social worker is pushing me to give her up for adoption. I can't. I love her so much." Sobs came as Rita tried to hold herself together. Marie went behind the counter and held Rita in her arms trying to comfort the distraught mom.

Deb spoke. "The Light will help you. The Light is Jesus. Mom can tell you about Him. The Light helped us."

Bobbie, said, "Light, Light." He held the new teddy out to Rita.

Marie looked at Bobbie. "Bobbie, I thought you were going to give that to Daddy?"

"Teddy helps," he said.

Marie's eyes embraced her two children. They were a team.

Rita bent down to Bobbie's level. "Bobbie, I can't take your new teddy. That's for your daddy."

Bobbie still held the teddy out to Rita and said again, "Teddy helps."

Rita took the bear and hugged both the teddy and Bobbie. "Thank you, Bobbie. You can all go to your daddy's room now."

Rick opened his eyes when they entered. "Hi … team," he said. Bobbie ran over and climbed up on top of the hospital bed next to his dad. Deb and her mom walked to his bedside.

Marie began, "It's so good to see you awake. Did Jane come to see you today?"

Rick nodded. "Dad … came … too."

"Really? That's wonderful. It must have taken some organizing to get Lee here."

Rick nodded.

Deb seemed to be waiting to get an answer to her promise that she would believe in the Light if her dad said a full sentence without hesitating.

Rick said, "Deb … I … love … you."

"I love you, too, Dad."

For the next twenty minutes, the Winton team sang songs, talked about special memories, and prayed. Rick was mostly silent, but smiled and held his family's hands. The four of them were truly a family team.

Chapter 27

BLUE LIGHT

Sleep came easy for Bobbie. Deb sat up for a while flipping the dial on the TV. She came across one TV show about midwives in the 1930s in England. These women, though not perfect in themselves were devoting themselves to saving babies.

Deb said, "I want to save babies when I am an adult."

"That would be wonderful."

"None would be allowed to die."

"Deb, all people, no matter how old, die at some point in their lives."

"Why did God make us, then, if we have to suffer and die?"

"God wanted a family of many children who love Him and want to be in His family."

"What if someone doesn't want to be in His family?"

"They have that choice, but then they will never experience the peace and hope God gives."

"I told Rita to trust in the Light even though I don't. It was all I could think of to say to her."

"You are my beautiful daughter. God created you and loves you. He wants you to stop fighting and find peace."

"Bobbie sees this Blue Light; You've seen the Blue Light; Dr. Willard sees the Blue Light. Why don't I?"

"Bobbie is totally innocent. He believes in the Light because no one has told him not to believe. I asked God to forgive me for the grumbling and for all the wrong things I have done. Dr. Willard trusts the Light with everything."

"Okay. So, if I tell the Light that I am sorry for the wrong things I have done, I'll see the Blue Light?"

"It's not a bargain or guarantee. You truly must be sorry. You must trust that the Light did give His life for you by dying on the cross and rising up alive, so you too can rise after your death to live with the Light."

"I'm scared."

"You can't cover up being scared with being mean, Deb. The Light will help you. He is always with us. He showed me the surreal ice so I could understand the wrongs that had piled up affecting our family. He took the ice away when I trusted in Him. I still sense the wrongs around me, but I understand that God loves everyone. He has created them and wants them to know Him."

Deb started to cry. "Is Daddy going to die? Will he always talk like he did tonight? Don't I have to be strong for Bobbie?"

Marie held her daughter in her arms. "Deb, you just have to be who you are. It is ok to be scared. It's okay to cry. It's even ok to be mad. The Light is around you. Wouldn't you rather have light than ice?"

Deb surrendered her determined façade and sobbed. "Mom, how do I connect with the Light?"

"Just start talking to Him."

Deb started hesitantly. "Light, I'm so scared and so mad about Dad. And about Mom having to work, and about school. Please forgive me for being mean. I don't know what to do. Please give us Daddy back. Please work out school." Deb was shaking with tears when a Blue Light appeared before them. The same hand that had reached out to Marie now reached out to Deb. Deb reached back and stopped shaking.

For the first time since Rick's sickness started, Marie saw peace in her daughter's eyes.

Chapter 28

SATURDAY

Saturday morning at 9:45, the Baptist school cafeteria began to fill up with people from the community. Dr. Hill was there. He came over and said hello to the Wintons and introduced them to another psychologist from Williamson, a small suburb of Beckerville. About 300 people were assembled by 10 A.M. When Dr. Willard walked in, several people including Deb and Marie wanted to jump up and greet him. Instead, they all simply clapped for him and his wife. Sally and Sarah came in at 9:55.

Deb surprised her mom. She got up and greeted Sarah and said three very special words: "I forgive you." The girls then embraced each other. Deb continued, "Please come and sit with us."

When Ruth and Howard came to the meeting, they also came to the table where the Wintons and the McCains were sitting. Marie was speechless.

Ruth said to Marie, "Thank you so much for loaning me your Bible and telling me about the Light, Marie. I believe that God has a purpose for my life for the first time in seven years."

"I didn't do anything special, Ruth, but thank you." *Praise to You, Light, for reaching Ruth.*

Howard sat down and sheepishly confronted Marie. "Marie, I don't understand this stuff about the Light or Jesus or this confounded ice, but Ruth is back and last night we had the best conversation we have had in ten years. I love my wife and I'm going to support her. And … um … I'm sorry about Rick."

Marie wanted to give Howard a hug, but simply touched his hand and said, "Thank you."

Ron and Jack and even Mr. Jacobs came in. This was unbelievable until Marie realized that Jacobs's Grocery supplied the refreshments purchased by donations from all the Beckerville churches. *Please open Mr. Jacobs's and Howard's hearts to hear about the Light.*

Marie's heart nearly burst when several people came whom she never thought would be at a meeting like this. Malory and her parents arrived. They did not make any effort to say hello, though Deb tried to get their attention. Meagan and Roger made their way to a table by the front. Roger was waving to everyone which is something Bobbie would have done. Deb and Marie excitedly waved back. Rita came in with a teenager. They both approached the Winton table. Everyone made room for them.

Rita announced, "Marie and Deb, this is Adele, my cousin. She is a student in the high school. Adele, this is Marie and Deb."

Adele spoke to Deb more than to Marie. "Deb, Rita has told me about your family and I heard about this meeting and asked Rita to bring me here. Kids in the high school are having the same problem. I became a follower of the Light last year in my junior year after seeing the surreal ice. My parents made me see a psychologist which really messed me up. I needed help and friends, so I secretly talked to Rita. She believes me. I want to help her with Alexandria if my parents let me."

Sparkling eyes and smiles graced the faces of almost everyone around the table. Deb reached out to Adele to touch her hand. "You can talk to me," Deb told her.

A disheveled man entered about a minute after 10:00 AM and slipped into a corner of the cafeteria. This was Carl! *Did he have any children? Why would he come?*

Pastor Barnet stood to start the meeting. "Welcome everyone. I don't think we have ever had this many folks in our cafeteria. Thank you so much for being here today. Our presentation and discussion will be recorded and aired on SFC, our local Christian radio station, at 7 PM this evening. A variety of pastries, donuts, and fruit are in the center of each table provided by Jacobs's Grocery and the area churches. Coffee, tea, hot chocolate, and water are available by the doors leading into the kitchen. For those who haven't helped themselves as yet, we will begin in five minutes. The bathrooms are located on the right side of this room."

Marie wondered why Sally got up to get another cup of coffee. She took the second cup to Carl, who snarled, "I can never get away from you being my waitress."

Sally smiled. "I can't help myself from serving one of my best customers." Her smile didn't fade as she returned to her seat.

Pastor Barnet stood again to get everyone's attention. "Today we have several area pastors and priests participating. I'll call Pastor Graves from the Nazarene Church to lead us in prayer." Marie's mind focused on his words which asked God the Father for wisdom, guidance, answers, and perseverance in the Name of the Light.

Dr. Hill was called to the podium. "A copy of the form from the middle school has been handed to each of you as you entered this room. It is a form that the school requires you to sign, but you can use a private psychologist rather than the school psychologist if your child is reported to have hallucinations. This is really about the surreal ice that some of you have experienced. That ice is not a hallucination, but rather a wake-up call from God. He reveals to us the wrongs in our lives and how to be forgiven and freed from those wrongs through belief in His Son, the Light. How many of you have seen the ice or know someone who has seen the ice?"

Almost every hand in the room went up except for Carl's and a dozen others.

Dr. Hill continued. "My colleague, Dr. Shelby, and I are setting up group therapy sessions if your child needs our help. There are no more than five students in each group. There will be one group from 6:30 to 7:30 PM every weekday night. Dr. Shelby will do Tuesdays and Thursdays. I will do Mondays, Wednesdays, and Fridays. These groups will meet at my office on McKinney Drive. At the close of this presentation, Dr. Shelby and I will remain at the table in the front to give more information and how to request one of us for your child's psychologist if needed. I suggest you put one of our names down before you sign the form. If more than 25 children need help immediately, we will open some Saturday meetings. Your child will probably only need to come to two or three meetings. It will cost $20 per session to satisfy the state that it is legal."

Malory's mom, Cindy, stood and yelled, "This is a rip-off! You are just trying to take advantage of these kids to make some extra cash!"

Pastor Barnet intervened. "Please sit down, ma'am. No one has to take advantage of Dr. Hill's offer. It is a very low fee and provides an answer to many of the parents gathered here today. You are welcome to discuss your concern at the end of our presentation."

Cindy sat down so hard that some people were concerned she might have hurt herself. Malory was turning a shade of purple.

Marie glanced around the room to see if she recognized anyone from the school district or local government even though she wasn't familiar with many in those positions.

Pastor Barnet then continued to address the gathering. "Yesterday, a talented woman from our community contacted me and presented an amazing plan to help our students. Some families are able to send their children to our Baptist school. Of necessity, we must charge enough to pay our teachers and maintain our facility. We realize that many families cannot afford to attend here and must go to the public school. That is not a bad thing as long as our children have the foundation they need in truth. Some of our children are the Light's messengers in the public school. Ruth Stanton, would you please present your plan to this group?

To Marie's surprise, Ruth, along with two other ladies, approached the podium carrying papers.

Ruth began, "We were Montessori teachers. The school closed seven years ago. The city has not been able to rent it or sell the building. I believe that is because the Light wants us to have it as a place of Biblical, historical, and scientific truth. I propose that we as a Christian community rent the facility until we are able to purchase it. It will not be a school like this Baptist school, but rather one in which students come after school. It is within walking distance from the middle school and high school. My fellow Montessori teachers here, Ava, Catherine, and I will compare the curriculum from the public school to Biblical teaching and historical facts contained in Biblically based curriculum from a variety of trusted resources. We will delve into scientific truths which either support or refute what is being taught at the public school. There will be open discussion and help with homework every day after school until 5:30 PM. On Monday evenings, a parent group will meet to discuss our curriculum from 7:00 to 9:00 PM. We will only ask for minimum wage at 20 hours per week to cover some of our prep time and teaching time. The facility will be open for us to rent to other groups during the day and on weekends. We just need to do our own maintenance and pay the rent, taxes, and utilities. The city is losing $8,000 a year on the property. We can get it for $1,000 per month with about $800 more per month in utilities and taxes. I believe that we can earn that much from those who rent the school during the week and on weekends. We will charge $25 per week per student and trust that some churches will give scholarships. Our children need us. My husband, Howard, has volunteered his construction company to give two days of service for getting the building ready. Many of you can paint and clean and help out in other ways. Please give this idea a chance. It could make a difference for every child in our community."

The entire room with few exceptions stood and applauded. A few voiced doubts. One young man ran to the podium. Pastor Barnet knew him. "Pastor Nichols, do you have something to say?"

"Excuse my exuberance! Our church has been meeting in Ray Huston's basement for eight months. We have been praying for a place to rent for Sunday services and Wednesday night programs. This is an answer to that prayer. We also have members who can help with getting the school ready."

The two pastors did a high-five and said, "Praise the Light."

Pastor Barnet spoke, "We must not leave this as an idea. You were handed another form when you came in. It says, 'Freedom School.' We are asking you to fill in this questionnaire. We have asked all the pastors and priests here today to go over these questionnaires with their congregations and send or deliver the information gathered to the address on the form. Dr. Willard, Dr. Hill, and Dr. Shelby all agreed to sign the rental agreement presented by the city once $3,600 is collected for the first two months. We'll have a collection today and will continue in our churches. As soon as the school is ready and the finances are provided, the school will open. We need to pray. Please gather with five or six people at your table and pray for this school to open and for the children in our community to come to know the Light."

About two-thirds of the people present gathered in groups to pray. Most of the others looked over the forms. A few got up to leave. Marie overheard one lady say, "That Ruth lady must be a new believer in the Light. She is expecting a miracle and miracles are few and far between."

Howard started to stand and face the woman who spoke against Ruth when he saw it: the surreal ice covered him. Carl, in the corner of the room, was covered as much as Howard. There was horror in Howard's face as he said, "Ruth said that the ice was gone!"

Sally spoke first. "Mr. Stanton, are you okay?"

"Okay?! I'm covered with this weird ice and so are some other people here. How can you dream of a school with this virus attacking? Where is that doctor?"

Marie said, "Sarah, go ask Dr. Willard to come to our table." People started turning toward Howard. Ruth saw what was happening. She quickly returned from the podium.

Dr. Willard spoke to Howard. "I'm Dr. Willard. I don't have any of my instruments with me, but I am willing to open my office now and help you out there."

Ruth answered for Howard. "We'll come. Thank you so much. Howard, I'll drive."

Howard didn't argue.

Sally, Sarah, Deb, Adele, and Marie prayed, each taking a turn. They prayed for the Freedom School to become a reality, for Rick to get well, and for Alexandria to be healthy. They prayed for Rita to have the help she needed and for her mom to come to love her granddaughter. They prayed for Adele's family to accept her faith and that they would become believers.

Deb prayed, "Help Mr. Stanton to know the Light."

It was just yesterday that Deb fought against believing. Now she is praying for a man she called mean. The Light changes lives.

Rita listened. She knew she was supported, but didn't yet believe in the Light for herself.

The meeting slowly began to break up as families filled out the Freedom School form, had private discussions, and signed up with Dr. Hill and Dr. Shelby. Carl remained in the corner.

Marie put 'Dr. Hill' on Deb's form and Sally did the same for Sarah. The four ladies stopped to talk with Carl on the way out.

Chapter 29

CARL AND RICK

Sarah was the first to speak to Carl. “Mr. Murphy, thank you for coming to this meeting.”

“What? Why are you thanking me? There’s always free food here when they open their doors. I don’t care about any school problem.”

Sally would not let Carl brush this little group off so easily. “Carl, your crusty appearance doesn’t fool me. There is a heart under all that surreal ice. This school is a long way from home, too far to walk for simple refreshments.”

Carl ignored Sally’s statements.

Marie tied to reach him. “Carl, Deb and I are going to see Rick at the rehab center. He would love to see you.” *What is causing Carl to be so gruff? Does he see the ice on himself?*

“They would never let me in that place.”

“We snuck my boisterous four-year-old in. I think we can manage getting you in.”

“Leave me alone.”

“No. I think Rick needs to see you.”

"What for?"

"You'll have to ask him yourself."

"Well, I ain't walkin' there."

"You can ride with us."

"Okay . . . Okay . . . just warnin' you, they won't let me in. Then you'll have to drop me off at Sullivan and Harris."

Deb rolled her eyes, but went along with her mom's idea. Sally and Sarah couldn't believe that Carl agreed to go. They nodded in a way that supported Marie's invitation. *Light, please help me with this. Please make a way for Carl to see Rick. I just know this will help both of them.*

Marie and Deb escorted Carl to the parking lot, and Marie opened the door to the front passenger seat. "Carl, you can ride up front with me."

Carl hesitated, but got in. Deb got in the back. The ride to the hospital rehab center was quiet while urgent prayers were mentally sent.

They met Jane, Lee, and Bobbie in the lobby of the hospital. This was to be a family visit. Bobbie ran to hug his mom's legs and Deb's legs. "Bobbie, did you have a good time with Nana and Papa?" Bobbie simply laughed joyfully.

"Jane, Lee, I want you to meet Carl, a friend of Rick's."

Lee wheeled his wheelchair over to Carl and offered his hand. "It's a pleasure to meet you. Rick needs his friends now. It's good of you to come." If Lee noticed Carl's appearance, he definitely did not reveal that to Carl. Carl was speechless, but took Lee's hand.

Bobbie then imitated his Papa and held his hand out to Carl. Carl did not know what to do. Bobbie touched Cal's hand and said, "Friend, friend."

Carl replied to Bobbie, "Friend."

The group proceeded down the hall, past the information desk, gift shop, and elevators to the rehab entrance. They were an unusual bunch; a beaming four-year-old holding the hand of a despondent, unkempt middle-aged man; a smiling sixty-year-old in a wheelchair pushed by a cheerful old woman of the same age with swollen legs; and an optimistic mom linking arms with a skeptical twelve-year-old. The group received stares, but no one stopped them, not even the clerk at the rehab desk. The whole menagerie simply entered Rick's room without a single complaint from anyone.

Rick was sitting up in bed. The first word he uttered was, "Carl!" Tears rolled down Rick's face. "Carl, man … I've … missed … you."

Carl walked over to Rick's bedside just as Bobbie dropped his hand and climbed up to be next to his dad.

Carl spoke in a hushed voice, "I'm sorry, Rick. You don't need to be like me."

"You don't … need … to be … stuck where … you are … either … Carl … That … murky ice … is from … us … it's from … complaining … from all … the bad stuff … we … ever did … or thought … It builds up … the Light … didn't … make it … We did … but … the Light can … take it away … because of … the Light."

Bobbie repeated, "Light, Light," and smiled that impish smile that no one could resist. He then crawled off the bed and again took Carl's hand, "Friend."

Marie sensed the fight going on inside Carl. Bobbie's innocence broke through the hard crust and Rick's effort to talk to him melted some clinging bitterness. Frozen tears clung to the corners of Carl's eyes.

Deb went over to Carl and took his other hand and said, "friend."

Then Lee spoke. "Carl, Rick is right. I was caught up in blaming God for all the negative things in life. I became grumpy and hard to live with. Just ask my wife." Jane nodded. "In fact, my bitterness and rebellion against God led to a stroke. That stoke put me in a wheelchair. Depression filled every moment of every day, and all I could do was watch TV. But then I saw a program about the Light and how to be free from my miserable condition. The Light is another name for Jesus because He brings Light into our lives and takes away darkness and that surreal ice. He put all the rubbish we carry on Himself and died for us so we don't have to live with that ice and darkness. He rose from the dead, too, so when we do die, we can be with Him in heaven. All we have to do is believe and trust in Jesus, the Light of the world. Carl, I have so much joy now even in this wheelchair. I want you to have joy, too."

"Why are you all doing this for me?"

Rick tearfully replied to Carl's question. "You were there … for me … when I … needed … someone …t o talk to … I love you … man ... I want you … to know … the Light.

Marie felt tears in her eyes, too, as she went to Rick and put her hand on his shoulder. "Carl. thank you for being there for Rick when I was not the one he could talk to. I love you, too, and want you to know the Light."

"How?" asked Carl.

Deb squeezed Carl's hand and said, "I'll help you. You just start talking to the Light. Tell Him you want to know Him and that you are sorry for things you have done that probably God doesn't like. He will answer your prayer."

Jane walked over to Deb's side and took her hand and Rick's. Lee wheeled next to Bobbie and took his free hand. They were all in silent prayer as Carl began choking out his words.

"I hear about you, Light. You look to be real with these folks. If you are real, show me and forgive me for all my insults to Sally, bitter judgment, and hurting my family."

The ice which had encrusted Carl for the last two years disappeared. Marie noticed a nurse who had just come to the door gasp as she saw Blue Light surrounding this unusual group. No one in the little room responded to the gasp. This was a special moment of silent awe and worship.

Carl exclaimed as he clapped his hands, "I'll be! This Light is real! I feel peace. Now what do I do? I know. I have to tell Sally. But, what after that?"

Lee spoke, "Carl, we go to a good church. Could we pick you up tomorrow? The service is at 11:00. Jane could actually use some help getting me out of the van."

"I'm not in a good area. Pick me up at the P&R Coffee Shop. I'll be there at 10:30."

Lee asked, "Can we drop you off there now? I would love a little lunch, and you could practice helping Jane."

Carl agreed.

Rick reached out his hand wanting to shake Carl's hand, saying, "Come back."

Carl took Rick's hand. These two men had a special connection.

Please, Light, protect Carl from doubting what you have done for him.

After Carl left with Jane and Lee, Bobbie got back up on the bed with his dad.

Deb asked her dad, “Dad, is your speech going to get better?”

“Yes. I’m … healing.” Daughter and dad hugged each other as Deb sat on the bed next to her dad. If there was any room left, Marie would have sat next to Rick as well.

Rick stated, “What a team!”

Deb then exclaimed, “Dad, you spoke a sentence!”

Chapter 30

JANE'S ACCIDENT

Deb, Marie, and Bobbie spent about fifteen minutes with Rick before leaving. They all were worn out. Sleep was more important to them than food, so they went home to take naps. Deb and Bobbie went to their rooms and Marie laid down on the couch. The phone rang just as her eyes were closing.

"Hello," she said without much enthusiasm.

"Marie, this is Sally. Jane has been taken to the hospital. Carl went with her. Lee is here at the coffee shop."

Marie's heart instantly beat rapidly as she stood up and asked, What happened?"

"She fainted just as she entered the parking lot. She only hit an embankment at a very slow speed, so, the van is okay. EMTs were here within minutes. They think she may have a clot in her leg that traveled. I called the hospital, but they said that you had left. I told the staff not to tell Rick."

"I'll go immediately."

"No, Marie. I'm driving Lee's van over to your house so that I can drop Lee and Sarah off. Then I'll drive you to the hospital in your car."

“That’s probably best.” They hung up with a short “bye.”

Why Lord? Everything was going so well. Jane was quiet when we were seeing Rick, which wasn’t like her. Please let her be okay. My Bible, I want to read my Bible. Ruth has it. I’ll call her.

Marie dialed Ruth’s number. She picked up on the second ring. “Marie, I’m so glad you called. Dr. Willlard was so nice. He checked Howard out completely and explained about the ice and the Light. I shared your testimony, too. Howard doesn’t want to commit to the Light yet, but he is physically ok. Dr. Willard didn’t push Howard at all and thanked him for volunteering to help with the Freedom School. Oh, and you’ll never believe this. At the end of today’s meeting, there were enough donations to rent the old Montessori School building!

Ruth’s excitement didn’t touch Marie’s heart due to her distress. “Ruth, are you home? I really need my Bible. Jane has been taken to the hospital.”

“Oh, I’m so sorry. I’ll bring it right over. Do you need help with the kids?”

“No. Sally is bringing Lee and Sarah over and then driving me to the hospital. I’ll be at the door when you come.” Marie’s words were slow in coming as more tears choked her throat.

Ruth was at the door in five minutes. She took Marie’s hand and prayed a simple prayer. “I know you are with this family, Light. Please give all of them peace and healing.” She hugged Marie. They had been neighbors for twelve years. Now a new Spirit united them as sisters.

Sally parked the van on the road next to the lawn. Marie went out to help with the lift. Lee was quiet as she pushed his wheelchair through the front door and into the living room. Sarah sat next to Lee.

Sally said, "Hey, I think Jane's going to be okay. Let's go, Marie."

Deb woke up with all the commotion. "What's going on?"

Marie answered, "Jane is in the hospital."

"What! Come on, Light, you can't let anything else happen to my family. Not my Nana!"

"Deb, Sally is taking me to the hospital. Lee needs to stay here. Could you be here with your Papa and Bobbie?"

"No. I want to go with you. Sarah is here."

Lee interrupted, "Let her come with you, Marie. I'll be fine. I'll play a game with Bobbie when he wakes up."

Sally encouraged them, "Let's go ladies. Marie, could I have your keys?" Marie gave Sally her car keys.

They made it to the hospital quickly. Sally parked in the hospital parking garage and asked where they needed to go to wait for information about Jane. Carl was in the waiting room when they arrived.

Carl stood as the ladies entered. Marie immediately went over to him and gave him a hug. "Thank you so much."

Sally spoke, "Marie, I'll leave your car in the garage. I can take a cab back to the P&R to finish my shift there. Would you like to go with me, Carl?"

"As long as you give me a good cup of coffee when we get there."

After Sally and Carl left, Marie took Deb's hand. "Deb, I'm glad you came." They held each other and waited.

It was a couple of hours before a nurse came to give them a report. "Are you here for Mrs. Jane Winton?"

Deb and Marie both said, "Yes."

The nurse continued, "Mrs. Winton fainted from exhaustion and dehydration. However, she does have a clot in her left leg which we are very concerned about. We need to get permission for immediate surgery to put in a screen to prevent the clot from moving to her lung. She is very fortunate to be here before the clot moved. We need a close family member to agree to the surgery because of her exhaustion."

"I'm her daughter-in-law. My husband, her son, is in rehab and her husband is in a wheelchair at home. So, will my signature be accepted?"

"I'll check with the doctor. I'm sorry for all your trouble." The doctor let Marie see Jane and sign the permission form, but Deb had to stay in the waiting room.

"I'll pray, Mom," Deb reassured Marie.

How did my twelve-year-old become a young adult in a few short hours?

Jane was responding to the IV fluids. "Marie, I'm so sorry. Is everyone okay?"

"Don't worry, Jane. The Light brought you here so the doctor could take care of the clot in your leg."

"But you need me to help with Bobbie."

"I need you to be well." Marie stayed with Jane for about ten minutes and read an encouraging verse from Isaiah. "So do not fear, for I am with you; do not be dismayed, for I am your God. I will strengthen you and help you; I will uphold you with my righteous right hand" (Isaiah 41:10).

When Marie returned to the waiting room, Deb was excited. "Mom, isn't the Light cool! He made Nana come here just when she needed to come. I know she is going to be ok."

"This is going to be a long wait. I don't have any money for food and I don't have much money left on my credit card. Will you be okay?

"Sure. You brought the Bible. We can study and pray and watch TV when we are tired." After 40 minutes, Deb turned on the TV. A couple other families came into the waiting area. Marie also called her home to give Lee an update.

Sarah answered, "How is Jane, and how are you doing?"

Marie gave the update and asked how Lee and Bobbie were doing.

"They are fine. Bobbie is giving Lee every book he owns to read. They just started playing a game and we ordered pizza. Don't worry. Howard came over from next door to help Lee with personal stuff and stayed for a few minutes. He said to call if we needed anything. We'll be fine. Lee also called his church's prayer chain, and I made a few calls, too."

"Thank you so much Sarah. I'm glad you are Deb's friend again."

"Me too. Can I talk to Deb?"

"Sure." Marie gave the phone to Deb. The girls talked for about twenty minutes. *How do they find so much to talk about?*

Deb was in better shape than Marie. *Why can't I trust more?* Marie's mind became full of anxious thoughts. *What if Jane doesn't fully pull through? Who will attend to her and Lee? Who will watch Deb and Bobbie on Saturdays? Who will take care of Rick when he comes home? Light, help me know what to do."*

Deb was sensitive to emotions. "Mom, what's wrong?"

"I'm just tired."

A delivery person came into the waiting room. "I'm looking for Marie and Deb Winton. I have two dinners for them."

Deb jumped up to accept them. "See, Mom, the Light will take care of us."

Marie apologized to the delivery person that she could not tip him.

He said, "I'm just happy to serve the Lord in this delivery service. May the Light be with you."

As the young man left, Deb said, "He was cute, too."

I did not see that coming. My little girl is growing up too fast. He was, however, a good-looking young man.

They opened the meals. They were from the Nazarene Church in town that Lee and Jane had started to attend. A verse, magazine, and puzzles were also in the box. The meals included lasagna, rolls, salad, cookies, water bottles, and a couple of granola bars for later. There was also a verse from the Bible written on a card. "Cast all your anxiety on him because he cares for you" (1 Peter 5:7).

This verse was exactly what Marie needed to hear. *Thank You, Light.*

It was evening when they were informed that the surgery went well. Jane would only be in the hospital a couple of days. Marie called to let Lee know. It was time for them to go home and come back tomorrow to visit both Rick and Jane.

Chapter 31

THE LIGHT'S ANSWER

When Deb and Marie arrived home, Lee was waiting with Sarah. Bobbie was in bed holding his lion.

Lee looked at his daughter-in-law and said, "Sit down, Marie. I need to talk to you." Deb and Sarah got the message and went into Deb's room so Lee could talk to Marie privately.

"Marie, you don't have to carry all the family's problems yourself. Jane has been doing too much, too. I've prayed and made some calls. I know that you and your mom and dad don't get along well, but they need to know what is going on, and as a Christian, it is your responsibility to demonstrate the Light's love to them."

"They can't babysit for Bobbie. They've never accepted him."

"Bobbie will be with you at the Becker School Monday through Friday. Deb will be in school. Rick will be at home for a while. Your dad is retired and really wants to help. He could be here with Rick. Your mom said that she will make two meals a week for your family until Rick gets back on his feet. Just think, you and Rick can be examples of followers of the Light. Your parents also might start to love and respect Rick and realize what a good man he is."

"That will take some time and courage."

"You're one of the most courageous women I know. You and Jane are a lot alike. I'm proud that you are my daughter-in-law—or I should say, daughter? Saturdays are easier than you think. We would love to have Bobbie and Deb at our home, but will need help. Guess who volunteered."

"I don't know."

"Carl. He used to have a family. His marriage broke up when he lost his job about three years ago. His daughter and grandchild moved to another state and didn't want a relationship with either parent. They were both killed in a car accident over a year ago. Carl blamed himself, but today, he felt that he has gained a family with us. He wants to help. He also really likes Bobbie, who reminds him of his grandson. He is a good man and a new believer. Kevin and Sophia will be moving here in about a month and can help, too."

Marie hesitated to respond as thoughts swirled in her mind. *I don't want to give other people the responsibility which is mine. However, the Light is putting other good people into my family's lives. Will I still be important to them, or will work hurt our relationships?*

Lee waited for Marie's response.

"Lee, I am overwhelmed thinking that it is up to me to fix everything and be there for everyone. Sometimes, I feel like a failure as a wife and as a mom because it was me who secluded myself and my children from the world. That seclusion hurt my marriage and sent Rick to find an escape at the P&R Coffee Shop. The Light has taken all this and turned so much around, but I continue to feel guilty and now Jane is in the hospital because of my dependence on her help."

"You always did what you thought was best for Deb and Bobbie. The surreal ice that grew in your lives led you and Rick to seek answers and help. That took determination. Look what has happened because you didn't give up. Carl, Rick, Ruth, Deb, and you have become believers in the Light through these trials. Always remember that the Light not only took away the surreal ice, the Light died to take away your guilt, too. He is putting His love in you so you can forgive others and yourself. Problems will continue, but the Light will be with us. We also have heaven to look forward to."

"Lee, you are amazing."

"So are you. How about getting some sleep now? Howard will help me get ready, and you can get the couch made up for my bed. I haven't slept on one in a while. This will be an exciting new adventure."

Lee called Howard, who came over and helped Lee. Howard asked about Jane, too, so he could report to Ruth. Howard said, "Call me in the morning and I'll be here."

After Lee settled down on the couch, Marie said goodnight to Deb and Sarah, who would spend the night, and slowly made her way up to her bed. Marie's life was different now, but better. "Thank you, Light for showing me the surreal ice that gave me the realization of the wrongs I committed against You and others. Forgive me for holding onto bitterness and guilt. Thank you for Lee, Rick, Jane, Deb, and Bobbie and for Ruth, Rita, Sally, Sarah . . . " Marie fell asleep listing names.

Chapter 32

A NEW MORNING

Diffused light broke through the frost-edged window. Frigid air woke Marie before the alarm. Marie slipped her feet out of the cold sheets and onto the even colder floor. *This could not be happening again*. The frost that edged the outside of the window frame shone like sparkling diamonds. The sight that met Marie's eyes as she looked out her window brought joy rather than dread. Neighbors were already outside clearing fallen tree limbs and putting salt on walkways. Kids were purposely sliding on ice patches. There would be no school today.

"Rick, get up," Marie yelled to her husband who lay in bed without moving a single muscle.

A loud "Mom!" jerked Marie to attention. Deb, her thirteen-year-old, stood at the bedroom door. "Bobbie wants to go outside, but I don't want to. Could you or Dad take him out? I just want to sleep longer."

Rick came up behind Marie and tickled her in all the right places.

Marie jumped, laughed, and pleaded, "Rick, stop it! Why don't you take your inpatient son outside?"

"I will … only if … you girls … make sausage and … pancakes for breakfast … This is a … celebration … No one goes to work … today."

By now, Bobbie was at the bedroom door with Deb. He shouted, "Pancakes, pancakes."

Rick responded, "Ice first!"

Marie waited with Bobbie and Deb in the hall while Rick quickly got dressed. Rick opened the bedroom door and scooped Bobbie up in his strong steady hands. He winked at Deb and said, "Pancakes … in one hour … Go back to bed … sweetheart."

Bobbie exclaimed, "Sweetheart, sweetheart."

Deb punched her brother in the arm.

Marie's jovial team went downstairs while she got dressed and did her devotions. The cell phone rang. It was Bennington Village where Lee and Jane now had a very nice apartment. Jane was on the line. "Marie, how are you managing in this ice storm?"

"Fine. Bobbie and Rick are in the winter wonderland outside. And that generator you and Lee got for us will make it possible for me to make pancakes for the neighborhood. How are Kevin and Sophia?"

"They called this morning and are fine. Carl called, too. He is over at the P&R helping to clear the parking lot and sidewalk. Mr. Townsend is blessed to have Carl as his maintenance man. Sally and Sarah are working at the P&R to provide coffee and sandwiches for line workers. They have a generator, too."

"Rita was supposed to have a test for Alexandria today. I wonder if she went."

"Call Ruth. Those two are amazing. You know that Ruth has unofficially adopted Alexandria as her grandchild. Rita's mom continues to have nothing to do with her own daughter and grandchild. We keep praying for the Light to change Rita's mom's heart and for Rita to know Him."

"Jane, you are a wonder. How do you keep up on all the news?"

"What else is an old lady to do? Besides, I like to know how to pray specifically. How are your parents?"

"The ice storm may keep my dad away for today, but he loves to visit despite my mom's complaints."

"She'll come around. Rick will eventually charm her."

"Keep warm, Jane. We'll hopefully come for a visit tomorrow. I think I should join the neighbors now."

"Go ahead, Marie, and may the Light shine through you."

"He has totally changed my life. I just hope the pancakes I make today don't damage my reflection of His love."

"They'll be perfect." Their conversation ended with loving goodbyes and Marie got ready to go outside.

Deb was up when Marie reached the kitchen. They both joined in the cleanup outside. Many of their neighbors did not have generators, so they were invited into the Winton home for sausage and pancakes. A couple of them brought frozen sausages over. Ruth, Deb, Marie, and of course, Bobbie, formed a pancake-making team. Deb's bedroom became the kids' hang-out while adults stood or sat in the living room and kitchen. It was tight, but warm and friendly. Even Malory's family came.

Marie thought back on her journey over the past year and raised thanks to the Light. *Here in my house were gathered people I had judged and had separated myself from. The Light gave me courage to face life, seek forgiveness, and accept the Light's leading. Joy and peace, which often made no sense, now fill my heart and mind. Only the Father of the Light and the Light Himself knows what lies ahead in my journey with Him, but it will be good.*

ABOUT THE AUTHOR

Dale grew up on a family farm and was fascinated by the shapes, colors and life in nature. As a child, she began to talk to God about what she saw and heard. Later those words became poems and descriptive words which filled the stories she wrote. Throughout life, Dale wrote poems for people, stories for children, and recorded experiences and memories. She researched and created Sunday School lessons and adult curriculum. She has started a website (dalewitkowski.com) to share what she has written.

Dale's love for nature also inspired her to draw, paint, quilt, and create sculpture. She has a BA and MA in art education. The thing she misses most in retirement is creating art lessons and examples. However, she is an artist and has created multiple banners for church and continues to draw and paint. One of her resent paintings is the background on her website. The background image on the cover of *Surreal Ice* is one of her drawings. Over her lifetime, individuals have hired her to do paintings of their homes or favorite scenes.

Dale can't remember a time that she didn't believe in God or Jesus, but she did not always listen to Him and made some decisions that were not good. However, she knows the love and forgiveness of God and He is most important in her life. She is a lay pastor in her local congregation, mission's director, prayer warrior, and sanctuary steward. She puts art and Bible verses together in the church windows and on a prayer board.

Dale also loves to cook and bake, but her four adult children are most precious to her. They are all miracles and all musical. One had a liver transplant at age two. Another had her entire colon removed as a young adult. Dale has two babies and one grandbaby in heaven. In all this, the Lord has rained miracles upon miracles in her life. She wants to share them with anyone who wants to read or listen.